Langley flicked a glance at Oscar. "Get the adhesive tape from the bathroom. We tie him first."

Oscar nodded and started for the open bathroom door. Langley motioned with his head at a heavy ladderback chair beside the sofa. "Sit down there, Rome."

I came away from the wall slowly, moving toward the chair.

Oscar went through the bathroom door and out of sight.

Langley's eyes and gun stayed on me as I moved toward the chair. But, for a few seconds, there was only the one pair of eyes. And only the one gun.

I snapped my arms down as I jumped sideways toward the sofa. The roar of Langley's gun filled the room. . . .

Also by Marvin Albert:

THE UNTOUCHABLES

Published by Fawcett Books:

Stone Angel Novels

STONE ANGEL

BACK IN THE REAL WORLD

GET OFF AT BABYLON

LONG TEETH

THE LAST SMILE

Gold Medal Classic Westerns

APACHE RISING

RIDER FROM WIND RIVER

MIAMI MAYHEM

Marvin Albert

FAWCETT GOLD MEDAL · *NEW YORK*

CAST OF CHARACTERS

Chapter 1

RALPH TURPIN LAY WAITING FOR ME ON THE FLOOR OF
my office. A bullet had smashed through his forehead and
destroyed the brain inside.

I took one slow, shaky step deeper into the room and
stared down at him.

My mind had gone numb. But it didn't require much
thought to realize that I was in trouble. The worst kind of
trouble. Everyone knew there was bad blood between Turpin and me. I could feel something settling around my
neck, tightening like a noose.

I wiped cold sweat from my face and went on looking
down at him, trying to think.

He was unreal as a waxworks dummy now. The abusive
violence and unclever trickiness that had been Ralph Turpin
were gone. He was just a bulky corpse in a shiny, shabby suit.

The blood that had trickled from the hideous hole in his
forehead past his wide-open staring eyes looked like a
dried rivulet of reddish mud. His lips were drawn back
tight as rubber bands in a grimace that showed most of
his discolored teeth. His stiffly curled hands lay on the
floor palms-up. His legs sprawled as though there were no
bones in them. His big .45 Government automatic lay near
his right shoe.

No reasons for his murder came to me as I gazed at
Turpin's corpse. But they would *have* to come.

Desperately, I stretched my mind back over the events
that had led up to finding Turpin dead on the floor of my

office. Events that had started with that phone call from him, just the night before. Friday night . . .

No icy shiver of premonition slid down my spine when the phone rang up on the flying bridge of the *Straight Pass* early that Friday night. I'm not psychic. I had no ghostly friend to whisper a warning in my ear.

I was in the cockpit of the boat in my bare feet, wearing dungarees and a pullover sweater, cleaning out the fish box in the stern. I had that good-guilty feeling you get at the end of a stolen day. It was supposed to be a workday, and I should have at least checked in at my office in downtown Miami to see if I had any new clients. It wasn't as though I didn't need the business. On that particular day I couldn't have put together enough of a stake to last me through two hours of bust hands in a dollar-limit poker game.

But I'd awakened to find a beautiful early March morning waiting for me—the sun warm, the sky clear except for a few patches of cloud scudding along before a northeast wind, the water just choppy enough. Perfect fishing weather.

I'd been unable to resist the temptation. So instead of driving to my office, I'd cast off from the end of my pier at Dinner Key and sailed out to the Gulf Stream for a day of fishing and skin-diving around the reef.

That's the hazard of making your home aboard a boat in southern Florida. Summer or winter, there's always that blue water of the open ocean out there, pulling you away from the tense, overcrowded land.

I won the *Straight Pass*, a thirty-six foot sports cruiser, in a crap game. The game ended a six-month losing streak in which everything had beaten me—the horses, the dogs, dice, cards. The funny thing had been that I'd sensed the bad streak was over the first time I wrapped my hand around the cubes in that game. The boat had belonged to the owner of a palatial Miami Beach motel—before I made six straight passes. Three weeks later, I'd lost everything else I'd won in that crap game at a Havana roulette wheel. I never again managed to hit it that big, playing small stakes against the odds; and I couldn't work up a big enough stake to make it by playing the safer bets for small percentage profits.

But I hung onto the boat, as an ace-in-the-hole in case my financial situation ever got really desperate. I added outriggers and a swivel fishing chair in the cockpit, renamed her the *Straight Pass* in fond memory of the way I'd acquired her, and moved aboard. With her big deckhouse and comfortable main cabin, the *Straight Pass* made a perfect home for a man. I could always take it with me when too much investigating of the undersides of people's lives made me need the healing solitude of the open sea.

I'd had a good day out in the Gulf Stream. The fish kept hitting with satisfying regularity, filling the fish box by mid afternoon. What little was left of my land tensions by then, I got rid of by going over the side in goggles and flippers, and nailing an amberjack and a hog-fish with the underwater spear gun.

It was evening when I sailed back to Dinner Key. I moored at my berth at the end of the pier, hooked on the lines for water, electricity and the phone, and sold my catch to people waiting along the dock. I fried a slab of tuna I'd kept for myself and made a meal of it. After washing the tuna down with a tumbler of brandy, I set about lazily cleaning up the cockpit, looking forward to that night's nickel-and-dime poker session with some of the other inhabitants of Dinner Key.

Then the phone rang.

I was feeling good, completely relaxed and pleasantly muscle-weary. I climbed the ladder to the flying bridge and picked up the phone. The voice at the other end brought me back to land—to things about the land I liked least.

"This is Turpin," the man's voice on the phone said. "How're you, Tony?"

"Fine," I said tonelessly, and waited.

My lack of enthusiasm didn't bother Turpin. "I'm

working as a house dick now,'' he said. ''The Moonlite Hotel. Know it?''

The Moonlite was in one of Miami's unsavory pockets of cut-rate gin mills and strip joints. ''I know it,'' I told Turpin. ''And its reputation. You must feel right at home there.''

That didn't bother him either. ''I need your help, Tony. Real quick like.''

''For what?''

''Show you when you get here. You can make it in twenty minutes easy from where you are.''

''Sure. But why should I?''

''I told you. Because I need some help.''

I didn't like Turpin. He knew that. But I still had the annoying feeling that I owed him something. He knew that too.

''Be there in half an hour,'' I snapped, and slammed the phone down, cursing myself for being soft in the head and letting Turpin spoil my evening.

I went down to the cabin, took a quick shower in the tiny bathroom, changed to a black polo shirt and a blue wash-'n'-wear suit. Pulling on socks and a pair of dark blue tennis sneaks, I left the *Straight Pass*.

Halfway along the pier, Jack McComb was waiting for me in the cockpit of his charter fishing boat. McComb always stuck pretty much to his boat, even when he wasn't taking customers out to fish. Ashore, his missing leg was a handicap, and he had to use crutches. Aboard his boat, using hand-holds, he was as agile and competent as any sailor. I told him I'd have to skip the poker game on his boat that night, and strode onto the cement dock walk. Old Mr. Cohen, off the yawl *Ibis*, was taking a last slow stroll for the night with his granddaughter. We exchanged hellos.

At the next pier, occupied mostly by middle-class families who lived aboard their vessels on pensions or the income from jobs ashore, parents were yelling at their kids to stop racing their bikes up and down the pier and come aboard for bedtime. At the pier beyond that, cocktail parties were in progress on several of the big yachts.

The dock area at Dinner Key always tugged at me when I had to leave it. It was a friendly, self-sufficient little community, made up of all kinds of people of different interests, incomes, ages—but knit together by a common, barrier-dissolving love of boating. You could find almost any kind of companionship you were in the mood for there, along with a way of life that got a hold on you. I rarely left the place any more, except for business or gambling.

Tonight it was business. What kind of business exactly I'd find out. One thing I knew for sure. With Ralph Turpin involved, it was bound to be dirty.

I got into my gray Oldsmobile, pulled out of the parking area, and drove north along the Bay Shore Drive into the nervous, noisy heart of Miami.

The girl sprawled across the bed was young. Not more than twenty-two. But she didn't look the way girls of her age and breeding were supposed to look. Not at the moment.

The odd thing was that despite her condition the breeding showed. And the youth. There was a not-quite-finished softness to the pretty, snub-nosed face, framed by the tangle of raven hair fanned out on the wrinkled pillow. Her figure, in a low-cut, rumpled black cocktail dress, was slim. So were her long, nylon-sheathed legs, revealed by the twisted-up hem of the dress. Her face, and the rest of her skin that showed, glowed with the even golden tan that is the badge of the year-round resident.

A girl like her didn't belong there, passed out on a bed in a cheap hotel, with an empty fifth of whisky for a bedmate, breathing harshly through a slack, lipstick-smeared mouth. Especially not a girl who could afford to carelessly drop a silver-blue mink in the middle of the not-so-clean rug.

"She came in early this morning," Turpin said. "Little after five thirty."

I turned my head slightly to look at him. Turpin was a

burly man, with stiff, thick gray hair cut close to his round, solid skull. His eyes had that peculiar emptiness achieved by men who've learned to meet your gaze directly without revealing the corruption of the thought processes behind them. His fleshy face was florid, with tiny broken blood vessels showing under the skin of his cheeks and nose. It was a year since I'd last seen Turpin. The year had treated him as badly as he'd treated it.

"Under her own steam?" I asked him.

"Uh-huh. But she was already pretty far gone."

"Turpin!" the hotel night manager snapped warningly. His name was Welch. He was a small man with a pug nose and a receding hairline that left a lot of forehead to furrow when he got worried. The way it furrowed then. "You don't got to tell every damn little thing that—"

"Yes, I do got to," Turpin informed Welch heavily. "We want Tony to help, we got to level with him."

He looked at me again. "The way I figure it, she musta been in some bar trying to drink herself under the table. Most of the bars close at five in the morning, and her still being able to navigate she must've bought that bottle and come here to finish her fun in private. She was plenty drunk when she checked in, but so what? Anybody could see she wasn't under age."

"Not," I drawled, "that it would have bothered anybody around here if she were."

Welch tried to rise in anger. "What kind of crack is—"

"Cut it out," Turpin ordered Welch. "Tony's right. I know it and you know it. And so does he know it. But that don't figure this time. This particular broad ain't under age."

I felt myself smile, stiffly, and unpleasantly. "Then why call me in on it?"

"Because," Turpin said, "we can't afford no trouble. Even if we didn't do nothing wrong this time. You know that."

I nodded slowly. The Moonlite Hotel got a lot of its trade from college kids shacking up with each other overnight and on weekend dates. I looked down at the girl on the bed again, felt an edgy, undirected anger rising inside me. Taking the hem of her black dress between my thumb and forefinger, I plucked it down to cover her knees—a meaningless gesture called forth by her vulnerability and by the things about her that showed through despite her condition.

I glanced at my wrist watch. It was a few minutes past nine P.M. "When'd the police phone?"

"About an hour ago," Turpin told me. "Missing persons. There's this guy up in Mayport, a big wheel. Name's Kosterman. His daughter left the house last night sometime, headed down here to Miami. He thinks. And he ain't heard from her since. So he gets worried, calls his local cops. They call the Miami police."

I looked at the plain gold wedding band on the finger of her left hand. "Strange it was her father. Ordinarily her husband would be the one calling around for her."

Turpin shrugged. "Maybe she's divorced, or getting one like half the broads in this town. Anyway, missing persons starts phoning all the hotels and motels here and in Miami Beach, asking for her. The routine. Soon as they describe her to me, I remember this dame. She signed the register Diana Jones, but that don't mean anything."

"Not here, it doesn't. You didn't tell the cops about her, I take it."

"Hell, no. The cops've been handing us enough trouble lately without us giving 'em something like this to bug us about. But when they rung off, I came up here to check on her. She didn't answer the door, so I just came on in. She didn't wake up when I shook her, so I had a look at the stuff in her handbag. Her right name's Diana Pines, like I figured. The name of Kosterman's daughter. So I had a talk with Welch here, and we decided to call you in. You're the cool kind. You can pull it off easy."

"It's not my kind of job."

"What the hell. You're a private detective. Like me."

"Not quite."

Turpin got out a cigar, stripped off the cellophane. He

mashed the wrapping into a tiny hard wad inside his fist, tossed it at the wastebasket under the dilapidated dressing table, bit the end off his cigar, and spat that into the wastebasket. I waited.

"Okay," he said, his anger under control. "So you've done better'n me since we split up. You don't have to touch some of the dirty jobs these days. But I know you a long time, Tony. You can do this for me. Just this once."

I grinned at him. "You mean for a favor?"

Welch, the little night manager, snapped: "For two hundred bucks!"

"Still not for me."

Welch switched his frown to Turpin. Without taking his empty patient eyes off me, Turpin clamped the cigar between his discolored teeth, lit it with a kitchen match he set aflame with a scratch of his thumbnail. It smelled vaguely like a damp, dirty rag burning.

"How's the old shoulder, Tony?" he asked me mildly.

My left shoulder, deep inside where the tiny slivers of lead were, began to ache on cue. Not sharply enough to require those little white pills I'd once needed for it, but enough to remind me. It was three years since they'd removed the slug and reset the smashed bone. But part of the bullet had shredded on the bone, and they hadn't been able to get all the fragments out. They remained to jog my memory, from time to time, of a hood named Velie who'd downed me on the roof of that freight shed. He'd been taking careful aim to finish me off with his second shot when Turpin rose up out of the shadows behind him and broke his spine with a .45 slug.

I drew a deep breath. "All right." I looked at Welch. "About that two hundred."

Out of the corner of my eye I saw Turpin grin smugly behind his cloud of acrid cigar smoke. He figured I was a sucker. He was right.

"One hundred right now," Welch was saying, relieved. "For just taking her out of here and getting her home to her father up in Mayport. The other hundred's for not mentioning where you found her. You get it after one week. If we ain't had no trouble from this by then.''

"Okay?" Turpin demanded of me.

I nodded. "Okay." I shoved my hands deep in my pockets and strolled around the bed, looking down at Diana Pines from different angles. It was none of my business, but I couldn't help wondering what had driven her to this.

Welch watched me, his forehead still corrugated with worry. "I only hope that Kosterman guy don't get some of his local cops to sweat it out of you where you found her."

"Tony?" Turpin forced a laugh. "Somebody'll sweat something out of Tony the day Georgia elects a colored Republican governor."

I looked at him. "You're as subtle as always."

He shrugged his heavy shoulders. "That was your department. Being subtle. We made a good team."

I went to the window. It looked down into a dark courtyard. A wide service alley cut from the courtyard to one of the side streets flanking the block.

"Bring her down the back way," I said, turning back to them. "I'll drive in and meet you at the fire-exit door."

I started across the room toward the hall door, hesitated briefly as I reached the silver-blue mink on the floor. I bent, picked it up, draped it at the foot of the bed. "Bring her gentle," I told them, and went out.

I'd left my Olds in front of the Moonlite Hotel. The red and blue of the neon hotel sign glinted dully against its dusty paint. I got in behind the wheel, started the motor, and let it idle in neutral. I got a Lucky out of the pack in my breast pocket, lit it, and took my time smoking it. People drifted past along the dimly lighted sidewalk, their voices reaching me with the odd contrast of accents you hear all over Miami City—Spanish accents from Cuba, backwoods accents from Georgia and South Carolina, Yankee accents from the Northeastern states. So different from just across Biscayne Bay in Miami Beach, where all the tourists fleeing winter make it sound

as if some New York or New Jersey city had been picked
up bodily and set down again on that strip of Southern
sand.

I continued to smoke for perhaps a minute. Then I
tossed what was left of the cigarette out the open side
window and drove the car around the corner.

I switched off the headlights as I drove through the service alley into the courtyard. Braking the car beside the
fire exit, I climbed out. The door opened, and Turpin and
Welch came out, carrying Diana Pines between them. She
was limp, her arms and head hanging. Except for her harsh
breathing, she might have been newly dead.

I opened the rear door of my sedan, picked the mink
wrap off her shoulders as they put her on the rear seat.
Turpin dropped her handbag on the floor beside her twisted
feet. When he pulled his bulk out of the way, I leaned in
and draped the mink carefully over her bare shoulders. It
was a cool night and with all that liquor in her she'd be
susceptible to infection.

For a moment longer I gazed down at her slack, vul-
nerable young face. Then I pulled back out of the car,
slammed the door, and turned to Welch.

The little night manager of the Moonlite Hotel was
breathing hard from helping Turpin carry the girl down.
Sweat beaded his face. I continued to stare at him. Finally,
he said, "Oh . . . yeah," and dug some bills out of his
pocket, counting them over to me.

I counted them again myself, and thrust them in my own
pocket. "This is Friday. I'll be expecting the other hundred in the mail next Friday morning."

"Sure . . . if you don't tell anybody where you got her."

Turpin said hastily, "Thanks a million for this, Tony. I
won't forget it. Any time I can do you a favor . . ."

"You can convince Welch here that it wouldn't be a
good idea for him to forget to send the other hundred." I
walked around the front of the Olds and slid in behind the
steering wheel. Snapping on the headlights, I backed the
car out through the alley into the side street, began driving
east to Biscayne Boulevard.

It seemed a routine enough little job that Turpin and Welch had asked me to handle for them—just return a rich little drunk to her worried papa.

Of course, a couple of the worst messes I've ever gotten myself into started out as routine little jobs.

But I couldn't know that this was going to be another one of them.

Chapter 2

MAYPORT WAS NORTH OF DADE COUNTY, ALONG THE coast. I drove up out of Miami along Route One, through all the little suburban communities of low-priced cottages, bungalows, haciendas and trailer camps, each nestled cozily in a luxurious stand of palm trees and semitropical flower bushes. The communities began to thin out a bit as I got farther away from Miami and crossed the line into Broward County. I pulled off the highway into the drive of a roadside tavern, hurried inside.

The phone booth was in the rear. I pulled up the Broward County phonebook, looked for the name Kosterman under the Mayport listings.

There were four Kosterman numbers. There was a Kosterman Ready-Mix Cement Works and a Kosterman Construction Corporation, a listing for Rudolph Kosterman, president of the Sun-Sand Development Company, and a residence listing for the same man. I called the residence number.

A man's voice, quiet and polite, answered on the second ring. "Kosterman residence."

"I'd like to speak to Mr. Kosterman if he's there," I said into the mouthpiece.

"Who may I say is calling, sir?"

"Tell him it's about his daughter."

"Oh . . . yes, sir," the man said quickly, and went away.

Three seconds later another man's voice, heavy and

12

frightened, came through the connection: "This is Rudolph Kosterman. What . . ."

"I'm bringing your daughter home, Mr. Kosterman."

"My . . . is . . . is she . . ."

"She's all right," I said soothingly. "Just fine, except she's had a bit too much to drink. Otherwise there's nothing to worry about. I'll have her home inside the hour."

"She's not hurt? Or . . ."

"Not damaged in any way," I assured him.

"Thank God . . . Who are you?"

"My name's Anthony Rome," I told him. Then I cut off further questions by asking exactly where I'd find him around Mayport. I could have guessed his answer. Most of Mayport sprawled along the west side of the Intracoastal Waterway, but there was a portion of it known as The Island that lay on the other side of the Waterway. The Island, formed by the waterway on one side, the ocean on the other, and a canal at either end, was inhabited exclusively by the big rich. Rudolph Kosterman lived on The Island.

I hung up and left the tavern.

Diana Pines was still huddled on the rear seat of my car, the way I'd left her. But she was beginning to stir and make vague sounds in her throat. I got in and drove north again, glancing back at the girl from time to time.

I'd covered another ten miles when Diana Pines suddenly sat up on the back seat, a choked whimper coming through her clenched teeth. Swinging the car off the road, I got out and yanked open the rear door. I helped her stumble a few feet from the car to a clump of bushes, held her head while she threw up.

When her last spasm passed, her legs became rubbery. I picked her up and carried her back to the car, eased her on the rear seat, got the Kleenex from the glove compartment and gave it to her. I waited while she used it. Her face was no longer slack. It was sharp with fear, her eyes wide and uncertain as she looked around her not understanding.

"You're on your way to your father's place," I informed her quietly. "Be there in a half hour or thereabouts."

She turned her head slowly and forced herself to look at me.

"My name's Anthony Rome," I told her soothingly. "You had too much to drink, passed out in a hotel room in the city. I'm taking you to your father. He was worried about you."

She continued to stare at me. A different kind of sickness crept into her large, dark-brown eyes. "Did . . . did I . . ." Her whisper was ragged and she didn't finish it.

I shook my head. "No. Not with me anyway. Not with anybody, as far as I know. You were all alone when I got there."

Some of the stiffness went out of her face and figure. She slumped back, head lolling against the cushion, eyes closing slowly. I shut the rear door, got behind the wheel again. As I pulled the Olds back onto the highway, I glanced back at her. She was slumped down in the seat again, sleeping. Her breathing was not so harsh this time.

A short drawbridge over the waterway connected the mainland part of Mayport with The Island. There was a uniformed cop in a tiny stucco guardhouse on the other side of the bridge. He stopped me and had a look at my driver's license, then let me into The Island. Kosterman must have phoned him to let me in. He glanced at the girl asleep in the back seat, but whatever he thought didn't show on his face.

I drove along the darkness of Surf Road, which twisted around The Island. My headlights picked out only the road and the palm-and-pine forest on either side of it. Somewhere in that lush forest were the homes of The Island's top-bracket, privacy-cherishing inhabitants. But except for an occasional driveway entrance, there was no sign of habitation from the road.

The Kosterman driveway entrance was flanked by two tall stone-and-shell pillars, each topped by a big frosted light globe. Two men stood waiting beside one of the pillars. The globe atop it shone down on their heads. When

I stopped between the pillars, they hurried to the side of my car.

One of them was tall and broad-shouldered, somewhere in his late fifties, with a tough, lined face and thinning gray hair. The other man was shorter and slimmer and much younger—about thirty. He was blond, handsome, and worried.

The young one reached the car first, glanced at me. Then his eyes slid to the rear seat where the girl, her eyes opening, was struggling to a sitting position.

He blurted "Diana!" and opened the rear door, reaching in for her. I watched her flinch away from his touch. He saw her reaction too, and his face got stiff. He pushed in and sat on the seat beside her. But he did not try to touch her again.

"Diana," he said softly, pleading, his fists clenched tightly on his knees, "we've all been goddamn worried. Where'd you disappear to?"

Diana Pines sank her teeth in her lower lip and looked away from him out the window, not answering. He looked at me. "I'm Darrell Pines. What's your connection with my wife?"

"I brought her home." I looked at the bigger, older man. He stood beside the car, his powerful shoulders sagging a bit, watching his daughter and son-in-law with a puzzled frown. "Mr. Kosterman?" I asked him.

He turned his head slowly, nodded. "You're the man who phoned? Rome?"

"That's right."

"How did you happen to—"

I interrupted him. "Right now you'd better get your daughter to bed. Let her sleep it off."

"Of course," Kosterman agreed at once. He got in the front seat beside me. "I've sent the servants to their building. I didn't want them to see. . . ." Kosterman let his words trail off, pointed up ahead. "Just follow the drive. Where it forks, turn left."

I let out the brake, followed the drive through a heavily wooded tropical park. At one point, on the right, we passed a large clearing containing four tennis courts flanked by two small stone buildings. Farther on, to the left, I spotted what looked like stables through the trees. I reached the fork and swung left.

The park gave way to a vast, beautifully manicured lawn, studded with sculptured trees and bushes. In the center of the lawn, sprawling over a slight rise in the land, was a long, low, rambling modern building of irregular stone, redwood siding, and glass. It was a ranch-style house, but large enough to contain any six ordinary ranch-houses without bulging. The interior lighting showed through the glass-walled areas revealed a number of separate gardens, enclosing individual terraces. To the side of the house was a good-sized private channel dock at which was moored a beautiful ninety-foot schooner yacht.

I swung past a six-car garage and pulled to a halt by a wide stone walk that led between rows of small palms to a heavy redwood entrance door studded with bronze nail-heads.

"Rome," Kosterman said quietly, "would you mind coming in with us? For a few minutes."

"Sure." We got out on opposite sides of the car.

Darrell Pines was climbing out of the back on Kosterman's side. He reached in to help his wife. Instead of taking the offered hand, Diana Pines opened the door at her side, stumbled out where I stood. She would have fallen immediately if I hadn't grabbed her arms and steadied her.

She swayed heavily against me, looked blearily up at my face, and muttered loudly: "Hi, pal. Take good care've me, huh?"

She was play-acting, for her husband's benefit. I glanced at him. Pines, his mouth drawn thin, was white with anger. But he didn't make another attempt to get near his wife.

The big front door opened as I started Diana Pines around the car. Two women came out. One stopped just outside the doorway, staring in our direction. The other hurried along the walk toward us. She was a short, deli-

ciously curved woman in her early thirties. Her light-
weight tweed suit was tailored to show off her body, and
her long honey colored hair framed a strikingly pretty,
rather sensuous face.

She hesitated briefly as she reached us, studying Diana
Pines, quickly judging her condition. Then she put her
arms around the girl and took her from me. "Come on,
honey," she said gently. "Come inside with me."

Diana Pines turned to her immediately, leaning against
her. Though Diana was less than average height, she was
a good two or three inches taller than the woman. "Oh,
Rita," she moaned softly, "I feel so awful."

"Sure you do, honey. Hangover. And I'm just the girl
who knows what to do about it."

Kosterman came over and helped her guide his daughter
up the stone walk.

The other woman was still standing beside the open
door, watching. She was tall and slender. The light from
the doorway behind her shone against red hair. She wore
a light blue cocktail dress, cut very low. She looked as if
she were in her middle or late twenties.

As Diana Pines reached the door with Rita and her father, the redhead forced a grin at her. "My God, Diana,
you gave us a scare. What happened to you?"

Diana Pines turned her head and looked at the redhead
with naked hatred. Then she went on into the house with
her father and Rita. I watched the redhead stare unhappily
after them for a second, then turn and look at Darrell
Pines. Pines kept his face blank, looked at me.

I turned back toward my Olds.

"Just a minute, fellow!" Pines snapped. "We'll want
to ask you some questions."

I looked at him. Pines was slim and smaller than me.
But he acted quite sure of himself. I kept on walking to
the open rear door of my car, reached in and got the mink
and the handbag. Pines had hurried up behind me. I
dropped the fur and handbag into his hands, strode past
him up the stone walk between the palms.

The redhead was still standing beside the open door

when I reached it. I stopped, looking at her. A spray of freckles crossed her cheekbones and the high bridge of her nose under her wide-set greenish eyes. Her face had a too taut look, and her features weren't small enough to be called pretty. But she radiated a very distinct quality of tense sex appeal, and the way she held herself revealed that she was quite aware of it. She looked back at me, her gaze as directly appraising as my own.

I motioned for her to go inside first. "I'll follow you. I might get lost in there."

The redhead grinned. "It's been known to happen." She led the way through a wide entry hall with a marble-tile floor and pecky-cypress walls covered with huge abstract paintings. Her walk was graceful, with smooth, controlled strength to it.

I followed her past a living room about the size of a luxury-hotel lobby, a gold-and-brown dining area almost the same size, a kitchen large and gleaming enough to accommodate twenty ice skaters. We passed another doorway that gave me a glimpse of a big, lung-shaped enclosed swimming pool, bordered by a wide lanai with its own barbecue, bar, dressing rooms, and dining area—the whole space walled and roofed with a rose-hued translucent plastic webbed by slim redwood beams.

The room we finally entered was a large den, dominated by a stone fireplace wall. Lush indoor foliage grew out of the stone wall and in the corners of the room, softening the stark quality of its modern furniture.

Darrell Pines followed us into the room, dropped the mink and handbag on the long, curved couch in front of the fireplace. The three of us stood there waiting and looking at each other appraisingly.

"Well," the redhead said finally, "could anybody use a drink? Besides me."

I shook my head. Pines didn't do anything but go on looking at me.

The redhead shrugged. I watched her breasts dance. When I looked up, I saw that she was watching my eyes.

I grinned at her faintly. She didn't grin back. But she didn't look offended either.

"How long have you know Diana?" she asked me.

"About an hour."

"Oh?"

There was another searching silence. Before any of us thought of anything to break it, Kosterman came into the den, his heavy, lined face troubled. "Rita is putting Diana to bed," he told Pines. "If you want to help . . ."

"I want to find out what this fellow has to say first."

Kosterman nodded, looked at me. "Won't you have a seat?"

"I haven't got that much to tell you, Mr. Kosterman. Your daughter registered in a hotel in Miami early this morning. She was drunk at the time. She got more so with a bottle in her room—and passed out. The cops called around for her. The hotel management called me in to bring her home to you. That's all I know."

"Was she alone?" Pines demanded. He sounded tough about it. But he was just trying to cover how upset he was.

I told him, "She was all alone. Just her and an empty bottle."

"This hotel she was in," Kosterman said, "which hotel is it?"

"A hotel that doesn't want its name mentioned. The management would rather not be involved in anything. That's why I was hired to bring her back to you."

"Hired?" Kosterman's frown deepened.

"I'm a private detective, Mr. Kosterman."

"Detective? I thought you said my daughter wasn't in any kind of trouble."

"She isn't. I told you. They wanted me to bring her here to avoid getting the hotel's name smeared in any way. I don't think they really had anything to worry about along that line. But that's why they hired me."

"I could call in the police," Kosterman suggested, watching my face. "You could be forced to tell the name of the hotel."

"I doubt it. But why go to the trouble? It's not the

hotel's fault that your daughter picked it to drink herself blotto in.''

"Mr. Rome," Kosterman said quietly, "you can certainly understand my concern. My only child vanishes for over twenty-four hours, returns in this condition. . . . Naturally I want to know if she's in some kind of trouble."

He ran a hand through his thinning gray hair. It was the thick-fingered, scarred hand of a man who'd done a lot of rough manual labor at one time. He looked at his hand as though he might be remembering that. The hand clenched into a wide, solid fist. But then it opened again and dropped to his side. "I'll pay you quite generously for any information you can give me about Diana."

"Why don't you wait till tomorrow," I told him. "Talk to your daughter when she comes around. Then, if you still think she's in some kind of jam, it'll be easy enough to hire me to find out about it. I'm in the phonebook. Captain Crown down at City headquarters will vouch for me. My rates are reasonable."

"How do we know," Pines demanded suddenly, "that you're who you claim you are?"

I got out my wallet, opened it. Pines looked at my license photostat. Kosterman did not.

"You may be right," Kosterman said at last. "I'll wait and talk with Diana in the morning. I may call you afterwards."

I put my wallet away. "Be glad to hear from you," I told Kosterman. "Good night, all."

I left the room and found my way through the main section of the house. At the doorway to the room containing the swimming pool and patio, I paused and glanced in to assure myself I'd seen it right the first time. I had. It was still there—all of it. Probably not unusual in a house like this; maybe each bedroom had one like it, along with its own private bath, dressing room, fireplace, bar, and billiard room. I went on toward the entrance.

I was in my Olds outside, starting the motor, when the redhead came out the front door and hurried down the stone walk toward me. A sable wrap was draped around her shoulders.

She stopped beside the car, looked in the side window at me. "Driving back to Miami?"

"Uh-huh."

"Mind taking me along with you? I don't have my car here, and I think it's time I went home."

"Get in." I waited while she slid into the front seat beside me. Her dress hiked up, showing her exquisitely curved thighs. She slammed the door shut, looked at me. Then she pulled her dress back down, but she took her time about it.

I let out the brake and followed the curve of the driveway.

Chapter 3

She didn't say anything more till I drove the car out of the Kosterman estate and back onto the road. Then she sighed and relaxed against the seat cushion. "It'll be a relief to get home. It hasn't exactly been fun and games out here."

"Where's home?"

"It's not. Though it's getting so I call it that. It's just a place to live." She told me the address—a top-tab Miami Beach hotel.

"Nice neighborhood."

"If expensive is nice," she said, "I guess it's nice."

"Been out here since last night?"

She glanced at me sharply. "How'd you know?"

"Your dress. It's not a daytime dress, and it's not what you'd have worn if you'd come out tonight to help them wait and worry."

"I forgot you're a detective. Diana and Darrell threw a party there last night. Diana ran off in the middle of it. After everybody else left, I stayed."

We reached the drawbridge. The cop at the guard hut touched the peak of his cap to me this time as I went past. I went over the bridge and onto the highway. The redhead looked out the window at the trees flashing by in the night. "I was worried about her," she murmured. "Diana's a good kid . . . and I guess it was my fault."

I drove on without saying anything, waiting. But she

22

didn't add anything to it. Finally I asked her, "Do the Pines live back there with Diana's father?"

"Yep."

"How about the blond—Rita?"

"She interest you?"

I smiled.

"She's Rudy Kosterman's wife."

I looked sideways at her.

"Not Diana's mother, of course," she said. "She's the second Mrs. Kosterman. He divorced Diana's mother."

"They seem to like each other, Diana and Rita."

"They do. . . . Smoke?"

I shook my head. She lit one for herself and puffed at it while studying my profile.

"By the way," she said, "I'm Anne Archer."

She waited. "You have one?"

"Rome. I thought you knew."

"I meant a first name."

"Anthony."

"Anthony like in Tony?"

"Uh-huh."

"Tony Rome," she said, testing the sound of it. "I never met a private detective before tonight."

"Now your education is complete."

"Kind of a dirty business, isn't it?"

"Yes," I said. "It is."

"How'd you happen to get into it?"

"A compulsion. I have one about earning a living. Maybe you've heard rumors about that kind of compulsion. Among the lower classes."

"Okay . . . so I'm rich. Why be mad at me about it?"

"It is not good manners to tell a man in a dirty business that he's in a dirty business."

Anne Archer sat up straighter. "Oh-oh. Guess I said the wrong thing again. I didn't mean to hurt your feelings."

"I'll recover."

"You don't like me much."

"I like you fine," I told her. "I like redheads. Especially ones with long legs and wicked figures."

"Well, well . . ." she murmured. She turned sideways on the seat, looking at me more fully. "I didn't think I was getting to you."

"Don't you usually?"

She laughed softly. "The desirable males at Miami Beach are awfully choosy. They can afford to be. We outnumber them ten to one. . . . This calls for a drink. Let's stop some place. I'll buy."

"There's a flask of brandy in the glove compartment."

She got it out. "You?"

I shook my head.

She unscrewed the top and drank from it. "Very good." She sounded a bit surprised.

"I like to indulge myself with the little luxuries," I said. "The little ones are the only kind I can afford."

"You don't have to keep leaning on how much poorer than me you are," she snapped. "It doesn't matter to me."

"It does to me," I told her.

"Snob."

She leaned her elbow against the top of the seat back and eyed me thoughtfully. "Are you married, Tony Rome?"

"Nope."

"Ever been?"

"Not ever."

"How come?"

I didn't have to spend much time coming up with an answer. I'd been around that track before, many times. "I've got a gambling fever to feed," I told her. "And I live on a boat and like it. A woman would have to be shy of good sense to put all her chips down on that combination."

She considered that for a while. "Still," she murmured, "there are women who like to bet against the odds . . . if they stand to win something worth the risk."

I shook my head. "Sucker bet. We'd both come out losers."

"I've got a sudden hunch about you," Anne Archer said. "You're afraid of women. That's really it."

"I've never thought so."

"Well . . . you're leery of us then. And that's the same thing."

It was close enough to the truth to keep me from answering.

She went on studying me for a while. Then she said, "I am. Married. Or was. It's almost *was* now. I found out he was playing the field. Men are such dogs."

"That why you're down here? For the divorce?"

"Uh-huh. Sweating out my six months' residence. I've only got one more month to go. A little less." She added bitterly, "Then I'll be free as a bird."

There was nothing to say to that, so I just kept driving.

"Didn't you have me pegged from the start?" she demanded. "A smart detective like you? There's so many of us down here. Isn't there something about us all that you can tell us by?"

"Uh-huh," I said. "Loneliness."

"Oh, brother," she murmured. "You sure hit it there. And do all the men down here *know* it!"

"Where are you from?"

"Detroit. Good old lousy Detroit."

"How long have you known the Pines?"

"Five months now. Met Darrell and Diana at a party my first week here. I got high." She paused and then added softly: "Like last night . . ."

She didn't finish it. She looked away from me and took another drink from the flask. Then she put the flask away in the glove compartment and leaned back in the seat and stared straight ahead through the windshield. She didn't say anything more the rest of the way.

I didn't try to prod any more from her. You get used to unfinished dramas in my line of work. You're always dropping briefly into the middle of people's lives, getting a sharp, disturbing glimpse of how mixed-up they are, and leaving them that way. It's a series of second acts, in which you seldom arrive in time for the opening scene or stick around long enough for the final curtain. I had a memory full of cliff-hangers about which I still wondered whether those hanging had finally managed to climb back up on solid ground—or had fallen to the jagged rocks far below.

I cut east to the shore above Golden Beach and followed it down through The Strip, with its endless rows of gaudy luxury motels lining both sides of the highway. Down the length of The Strip and into the canyon of Miami Beach's Collins Avenue—with its mass of plush white hotels, cleverly illuminated at night to look like a hashish dream of an Arabian Nights' paradise. The swish of tires on the asphalt sounded like millions of hundred-dollar bills changing hands.

It was pretty late when we reached Miami Beach. But there was still plenty of action along Collins Avenue. Men and women wearing their best clothes and their proud new sunburns drifted between the hotels and the night clubs that crowd the street. For the stronger tourists, Miami Beach is a town where there is no end to one day and no beginning to another. The days and nights just go round and round, interrupted only by haphazard cat naps whenever the legs start to buckle with exhaustion. They come down there for fun, they pay through the nose for it, and their time is limited. They hate to waste a moment of it sleeping.

I pulled the Olds up to the entrance canopy in front of Anne Archer's hotel. Beside me, she straightened, hugging the sable wrap tighter around her shoulders, and studied me.

"I could ask you up to my suite for a drink," she said quietly. "But I don't think I will. I've done too much of the pursuing down here. It's not healthy for my ego. I just decided that. Just now."

I couldn't help feeling sorry for her. And she *was* damned attractive. "Go easy on yourself," I told her. "You haven't been doing anything unusual for Miami Beach. It's a common symptom of something we call the Divorcee Blues. You'll get over it."

"Ugh! You make it sound like post-pregnancy depression."

"There is a similarity. And neither lasts."

She shook her head slowly. "Still . . . I don't think I will ask you up. I'm beginning to dimly remember something from Detroit. Men act better if you let them do the pursuing. At least Detroit men do."

"We're pretty much the same, one place or another."

"Unfortunately." She got out of my car, onto the pavement, and slammed the door shut after her. Looking in at me through the open window, she told me quietly, "If you *are* interested, give me a call sometime."

She turned on her high heels and walked quickly across the pavement. A uniformed doorman appeared from nowhere, opened the big rose-tinted glass door for her. After she went through it, I let out the brake and drove away, feeling vaguely depressed and eager to get back to the *Straight Pass*.

I followed Collins down to Fifth and went over the Mac-Arthur Causeway to the mainland, skirting southeast Miami to take the Bay Shore Drive back down to Dinner Key. I began to feel better as soon as I got out of my car and onto the docks. It was quiet and dark there, and I could see millions of stars crowding the sky. Lights showed on some of the big yachts. The sea air's fresh tang filled my lungs and cleared my brain. On one of the dark vessels along the family pier, a baby began to cry but soon stopped; the gentle rocking of a moored boat and the sound of water lapping at the dock pilings add up to the most effective baby soother there is.

My sneaks made little sound on the timbers of my pier. I was halfway along it when I saw the man sitting in the outdoor phone booth near the end of the pier. He was not making a phone call. Just sitting there waiting, with the glass door open to get the air.

As I drew even with the booth, he stood up and came out of it. He was a paunchy man of medium height in a wrinkled white suit and a blue straw hat. He had a thin, pointed nose, pale eyes that had never liked anything they'd seen of the world, and a small mouth like a locked purse.

"You Anthony Rome?" He had the voice of the chronic whisperer.

I nodded.

He jerked a thumb at the *Straight Pass*. "Your boat?"

I said it was.

"I gotta talk to you, private."

I didn't know at the time that I had anything to be nervous about. I'd had a few desperate would-be clients seek me out there in the middle of the night before. I assumed he was one of those.

"Sure," I told him. "Come on board."

I stepped down off the pier into the cockpit of the *Straight Pass*. He climbed down behind me. I went to the light switch behind the flying-bridge ladder, flicked it. It lighted a small lamp in the deckhouse and a larger one up in the main cabin.

Just inside the open cabin door another man stood facing me with a gun in his hand.

This man was short and thick-bodied, with immense shoulders and a wide, brutal face that looked as if it had been stepped on gently by an elephant. The gun in his massive hand was a .38 Police Special with a silencer attached to the barrel. The dark, deadly little snout of the silencer was aimed at my stomach. The gun didn't quiver even a little bit. Nothing about the man moved.

Even his lips hardly moved when he spoke. "Come on in."

I looked from the gun to his tiny cold eyes.

The man behind me whispered, "You better. He don't look it, but he gets nervous."

I moved slowly through the dockhouse. The massive gun toter backed deeper into the cabin, keeping the gun aimed at my middle. I entered the cabin. The man behind me followed, but he wasn't quite close enough for me to be able to get away with whirling and grabbing him. Not with that gun trained on me.

The man with the gun tilted his head slightly at the canvas-and-hardwood yacht chair beside the transom settee. "Sit."

I lowered myself tensely onto the canvas seat, still watching the massive hood's gun and his eyes.

The voice of the man behind me whispered. "Put your left arm behind the chair. Just the left arm."

I felt myself stiffening. "Do I get told why?"

"I could shoot you," the short, wide man in front of me suggested thickly. "It wouldn't hardly make any noise at all."

He meant it. They both meant it; they wouldn't mind a bit.

I got my left arm behind the chair. The whisperer's hands seized my wrist, forced it down, taped it quickly and tightly to one of the chair legs.

"Now the right arm."

I did as I was told. My right wrist was taped securely to the other chair leg. Then the hands left me. I started to turn my head to look at the man behind me.

A large sopping sponge came against my face, smothering my nose and mouth and obscuring my vision. I held my breath as the first whiff got up my nostrils.

"Don't do that," the voice of the man behind me whispered peevishly. "I could easy knock you out first."

I fought down panic, made myself relax. I began to breath in the chloroform fumes. They went up my nostrils and filled my mouth and seeped into my brain. . . .

Everything began to blur and shift. My body detached itself from my head and floated away. My brain spun and kept spinning till it found a way to get out of my head and escape into darkness. Its place inside my skull was filled with the chloroform-soaked sponge. After that only my lungs remained, pumping like bellows. Soon there was nothing. . . .

Chapter 4

TANGERINE WAS STANDING ON MY LAP, LICKING MY FACE. I unglued my eyes and looked at him. He stopped washing my face and stared back.

He was a long, skinny, battle-scarred tomcat, with patches of fur missing that would never grow back and a chewed-off ear that gave his face a one-sided, rakish expression. I'd named him Tangerine because of his color. He wasn't a pet. He was strictly a waterfront freebooter. But we'd struck up a wary sort of acquaintance. When pickings were lean elsewhere or it rained or the sun got too hot, he sometimes came along the pier and down into my boat.

The weather was mild and there'd been plenty of fish leavings along the docks that evening, so it must have been a yen for milk that had brought him that night. He wasn't the lap-sitting and face-licking type ordinarily; the sight of me motionless on that yacht chair with my head hanging must have upset him considerably.

I raised my chin off my chest and mumbled: "I didn't know you cared."

As soon as I spoke Tangerine jumped off my lap and slunk away to a dignified distance. He uttered the growl that passed for a meow in his circles, then sat back and watched me.

The two men who'd ambushed me were gone. They'd left the cabin a mess. The shelves had been emptied of books. The lockers had all been opened and the clothes

30

and gear from them were now scattered over the desk. The cushions had been pulled from the settee and the mattress and pillow dumped from the forward bunk. The hatches were off the water tanks. Beyond the bookcase I could see that the galley had gotten the same treatment. Every jar and open container had been searched, the contents dumped. The icebox was open and its cake of ice was melting on the galley deck.

They'd searched me too, emptying my pockets and scattering their contents around my feet which were now bare. They'd pulled off my sneaks and socks.

It took me five minutes of pushing and pulling to work my wrists free from the tapes that bound them to the chair legs. They'd done a hasty job with the tapes, making them just secure enough to hold me while the chloroform was being applied. I stood up, stretched, rubbed my face with my tingling hands and looked at my wrist watch. I'd been out for an hour. Which meant they'd given me extra doses of the chloroform from time to time. My brain felt numb and a bit swollen, but otherwise I didn't feel bad.

I went to the galley, picked up the melting ice block and stuck it back into the icebox, shutting the door. Out in the deckhouse I put the engine hatch back in place, then prowled topside. They'd done a thorough stem-to-stern job. Some of it was just a matter of straightening up and cleaning. But there was real damage, too. My gorge rose but I knew I was going to get still angrier when I had to pay the repair bills. Up on the flying bridge there was more of it. The ship-shore radio had been ripped open. They'd even unscrewed the mouth-and earpieces of the phone.

The sight of all the mess and clutter combined with the fumes still in my brain to make me dizzy. I went up to the bow deck, stripped, and dove overboard, submerging completely under the surface. The icy cold of the water clamped me in a tight grip, but I stayed under, stroking away from the pier, as long as I could. Then I surfaced, gasped my lungs full of air, and dove under again. Surfacing again, I swam back to the *Straight Pass*. I was shivering violently as I climbed back on board, but my head was completely clear.

Toweling myself quickly in my cabin, I dug out my dungarees and sweater from the mess and got into them. Tangerine was still sitting there, eying me impassively and waiting.

I went to the galley, poured some milk in a saucer on the deck for him, poured myself a snifter of brandy, and took the glass with me out to the cockpit. Setting the cushion back on the fishing chair, I sat down and sipped the brandy and tried to sort matters out in my mind.

The earpiece and mouthpiece of the telephone had been unscrewed, so what they'd been hunting for was small enough to fit in there. Something smaller than the palm of my hand . . .

Tangerine, licking drops of milk off his chops, padded out through the deckhouse. He stopped a few feet from me and eyed me uncertainly.

"I'm okay," I told him.

He turned and made it from the deck of the cockpit up onto the pier in one effortless leap, stalked off into the shadows along the dock walk.

I sat there alone awhile longer, taking my time with the brandy till I'd finished it. I couldn't come up with an answer to what they'd been searching for—or even who *they* were. But I calmed down enough to begin the irritating task of straightening up the mess they'd made.

It took me two hours. By the time I was finished, I was mad all over again. Opening the settee in the cabin, I stretched out on the double bed it formed and pulled down my copy of Coxere's *Adventures by Sea*. I read two whole chapters of the seventeenth-century sailor's narrative before I finally simmered down enough to fall asleep. . . .

The first thing I thought of when I awoke in the morning was my twin Chrysler Crown engines. The engine hatches had been off, and they could have done a lot of damage without even trying when they searched there. I swung off the bed and went to test them. The engines turned over and started with no trouble. Breathing a sigh of relief, I cut them. After a quick morning swim, I showered, shaved, had three cups of black coffee, and got into my city clothes. Then I went down the pier to my car.

The hubcaps lay beside the wheels. I banged them back in place, got the cushions back on the seats and stuffed the strewn contents of the glove compartment back inside it. They'd probably been under the hood too. I got in behind the wheel and tried the motor; it worked.

Swinging around to the marine service station, I asked Ferguson there to check on the *Straight Pass* and estimate the cost of repairs. Then I drove to my office, which at that time was on the fifth floor of the Miller Building, near the junction of Miami Avenue and Flagler Street. I knew what I'd find by then, and I wasn't wrong. The door lock had been forced and both rooms—the small waiting room where I kept the files and the larger main office—had been searched. They'd done a fast, sloppy job of it.

I spent that Saturday morning putting everything back in order. The files were the worst job. I was itching to meet those two characters again by the time I got the folders back in sequence. But nothing was missing.

I didn't waste much thought that morning on what it could have been they'd been hunting. I had no idea. But I had an idea I'd find out.

Somebody thought I had something I didn't. I'd been searched—so had my car, boat, and office—and it hadn't been found. The way things like that usually went, it wasn't likely to end there.

I finished tidying up my office and went out to lunch.

When I came back, Diana Pines was waiting for me.

She sat erect on the early American bench in my reception room, her slim hands clutching a small handbag on her lap. The handbag was the same dark golden brown as her high-heeled shoes. Her straight skirt and simple high-necked blouse were in lighter shades of the same color—a color that went well with her wide, innocent brown eyes.

She was young enough to have slept off all signs of her

binge. A gold band at the nape of her neck held her black hair in a pony tail that made her look even younger.

She stood up quickly as I came in. "Mr. Rome?" Her eyes held no recognition.

I nodded. "How're you feeling today?"

A light blush suffused her softly rounded cheeks, and she sucked her lower lip back between her small white teeth. "I'm fine," she mumbled. "Thank you."

I took her into my office, settled her in the leather wing chair beside my desk and sat behind my desk in the swivel chair.

"I may as well admit right off," she said, forcing herself to meet my gaze, "that I don't remember you at all."

"S'all right. I didn't expect you would."

"My father and my stepmother told me about you. That's how I happen to be here." She'd spoken haltingly. Now she stopped and searched for more to say.

I nodded and smiled at her meaninglessly. It seemed to encourage her.

"I suppose I should thank you for getting me home safely."

"I was paid for it."

She eyed me hesitantly, chewing her lower lip some more. Then she blurted it out, "I want my pin back."

"Pin?"

She was caught between anger and embarrassment. "I was wearing it on my dress when I left home the night before last. It was gone when you brought me home last night."

It hadn't been on her dress when I'd seen her in the Moonlite Hotel. "What's this pin look like?"

Her mouth became impatient. "It's made of gold and diamonds in the shape of a daisy."

I put out my hand, knuckles down on the desk. "Is it smaller than the palm of my hand?"

"Yes. You do know what it looks like, don't you?"

I shook my head. "I didn't steal it, Mrs. Pines."

"I don't *care* who took it. I just want it back. I'll pay for its return."

"Don't you have it insured?"

"My father does. It was a present from him. Why?"

"The thing for you to do is notify the police and your insurance company. In that order. If the police can't find it, you can buy another, and the insurance company will pay the tab."

Her frown was uncertain. "I didn't think you'd suggest my going to the police."

"I told you I didn't take it."

Her shoulders slumped a little, and another blush warmed her face. "I . . . all right, I apologize. But I still want the daisy pin back. Without the police or the insurance company. I want *you* to find it."

"Why?"

"I don't want my father to find out I lost it. He's upset about me enough as it is. I don't want to worry him any more. Can you get it back for me? I'll pay you well."

"How much?"

"Would three hundred dollars be enough?"

"We'll see. I might have to buy it back for you. The same as the insurance company might have to do. Only if you took it to them *they'd* foot the bill."

"I told you. I don't want my father finding out and getting all unhappy about it. I talked to Rita—my stepmother—about it this morning. She agrees with me."

"All right. How much is this daisy pin worth?"

"About three thousand dollars."

"When was the last you definitely remember that you still had the pin?"

"I was wearing it on my dress when I left home and came to the city. I went first to the bar at the Drake. You know it?"

I nodded. The Drake was one of the city's best hotels.

"I was at the Drake bar for a long time. I remember that much. So I must have been wearing the pin while I was there."

"It might have fallen off without your noticing."

She shook her head emphatically. "It couldn't have just dropped off. It pinned very securely, with a lock catch."

"Were you alone at the Drake?"

"Yes."

"And after the Drake?"

She bit her lip and looked down at the handbag clutched on her lap. "I don't know," she murmured. "I must have had an awful lot to drink at the Drake. I remember the barman suggesting I'd had enough, and I didn't agree with him. I—I guess I was pretty nasty to him. Anyway he kept on serving me. After that, it all gets fuzzy in my mind. I can't even remember leaving the Drake."

"You don't know where you went next?"

"I don't remember anything else clearly until I woke up at home. Makes it real easy for you, doesn't it? I could have been anywhere. Done anything . . ."

"It's not as difficult as you make it sound," I told her. "I have the Drake and the hotel where I got you. I trace your movements backward from the one and forward from the other till I fill the gap between them."

Her mouth began to tremble. "That should be delightful for you. A drunk's progress."

"Don't be so hard on yourself. Most of us tie one on sooner or later.

"*I* never have." Her eyes were loaded with misery.

"Well, you have now," I said gently. "How much cash did you find in your purse this morning?"

"Six dollars. And some change. Why?"

"How much did you have when you left home two nights ago?"

"I don't know exactly. It must have been over a hundred." It hit her then. "My God! Did I drink *that* much?"

"Can you come back here around five o'clock?"

"You think you can get my pin back by then?"

"We'll see," I said. "Five o'clock. And don't start crying. Your mascara'll run."

After she had gone, I sat there awhile drumming my fingertips on the edge of the desk and considering. A three-thousand-dollar pin didn't seem to justify the kind of trouble and risk the two men with the chloroform sponge had taken. In fact, it wasn't at all likely.

I was getting up to leave when my phone rang. On weekdays Margo, in Ben Silver's office next door, took all my calls on the extension I'd had put through from my phone. Ben was my lawyer, and it had been his idea since I didn't need a full-time girl. I paid part of Margo's salary in exchange for her taking care of my typing and filing in her spare time and handling my phone calls. But neither Margo nor Ben would be in on a Saturday. I picked up the phone on the second ring.

It was Rudolph Kosterman, calling from Bridesberg.

"You told me to check on you with Captain Crown," Kosterman said over the phone. "I did. I didn't realize you were *that* Anthony Rome."

I stiffened, and a flash of an old anger came back to me as fresh as if the five intervening years had been wiped away.

"I knew your father slightly," Kosterman was saying. "I met him a few times in the city."

"My father knew a lot of big-money men," I snapped. "Too many."

I'd worshiped him. What had happened five years before had hit me hard but it hadn't changed that. He'd been a captain then, in charge of the police commissioner's special squad investigating racketeering connections. He dug too deep and scared too many influential people. They'd done some digging of their own. And they'd turned up proof that way back when he'd been a detective sergeant he'd taken a large bribe to suppress evidence against a rich man's son who was involved in a hit-and-run.

The first I knew of it was when I read it on the front pages of the evening newspapers. By the time I got to my father it was too late. He'd already put the bullet through his brain. I was a lieutenant on Captain Crown's armed robbery detail then, and the reporters rushed over for quotes. I gave them an earful. At the time he'd taken that bribe my mother had been going through her long final siege in the hospital, and I'd been about to start college. I told them what I thought of a city that paid a detective— three times cited for bravery—so little that he couldn't even secure a loan to pay for his dying wife's hospital expenses and his son's education. Then I'd handed in my resignation from the force before the commissioner had time to ask me for it.

"I didn't bring it up," Kosterman said, "to reopen old wounds."

"Then why bring it up at all?"

"Because it means that you understand how it feels to have someone dear to you in trouble."

"If we're talking about your daughter, Mr. Kosterman, let's keep it to her. She's not connected with my father in any way."

"Very well, Rome. I admit I was trying to get your sympathy. I had that talk with Diana this morning. She claims not to know where she was or what she did. And she wouldn't tell me why she left here in the first place. She's quite troubled about something. I know her well enough to know that."

"You want me to find out what's troubling her."

"Yes. I've spoken to her husband, and he has no idea what's bothering her. And now she's gone off somewhere again. She left right after I talked with her without a word about where she was going. She hasn't returned."

"Maybe your son-in-law knows where she went."

"No. Darrell is at the development office cleaning up a load of extra work. He left before she woke up this morning."

"Your son-in-law works for you?"

"He's vice-president in charge of sales for our development villas. Rome, I want you to find Diana. If you can."

"I can," I told him. "Then what?"

"Find out what she's up to, what kind of trouble she's gotten herself into."

"People get moody sometimes without being in any particular kind of trouble."

"If that's the case, I want to know it. To relieve my mind. Do you want this job or don't you?"

I did, and told him so. I was already estimating what

making him happy could mean to me. Kosterman was a top-income-bracket permanent resident of southern Florida. That could mean bringing my own income bracket up a notch—if he was satisfied with my work enough to begin recommending me to his coin-heavy friends and business contacts. One part of my mind began considering how those fat fees could buy me a long Caribbean cruise in the *Straight Pass*. But the gambler in me was dwelling on thoughts of an all-out assault on Las Vegas. . . .

I gave it some fast, careful thought before naming a fee to Kosterman. I had to make it low enough so he wouldn't feel he was being taken but high enough so he'd respect me—a ticklish tightrope you've always got to walk with the rich.

We settled on his mailing me a check to cover fees and expenses for the next few days. Then I left the office, took the self-service elevator down, and went to see Ralph Turpin.

Chapter 5

"THIS'S LIKE OLD TIMES," TURPIN SAID, LOUNGING BACK in the easy chair in his room on the second floor of the Moonlite Hotel. "Seeing this much of you. Nice." He chewed the stub of his unlighted cigar and eyed me warily. With his jacket off I could see that some of his weight had gone to fat in the past year. But I still wouldn't have wanted to go any rounds with him.

I sat on the edge of his bed, got out a pack of Luckies, and lit one. "It's hard to stay away. Your company's so stimulating."

"You ain't changed at all. I told Welch you'd get the girl back to her old man without a beef."

"What makes you think there's no beef?"

"I'd've heard the squeal by now."

"You're hearing it now. She wants the daisy pin back."

He tongued the dead cigar butt from one corner of his mouth to the other. "The which?"

"The pin you took off her dress. Gold and diamonds in the shape of a daisy."

His eyes might have been watching a blank TV screen, waiting for the picture to come on. "You got a real high opinion of me."

I shrugged. "Like you said last night, I know you a long time. That's why I bought you out of the agency."

"You're knocking on the wrong door. I didn't lift anything off her."

"Sure you did," I told him mildly. "The pin and some

40

dough out of her purse. When you went up to her room to check her identity. She didn't answer your knock, so you let yourself in and saw she was out cold. You pocketed most of her cash while you were looking for her identity. And then you took the pin off her dress. She doesn't care about the cash. Just the pin.''

"Drunks're all the same," Turpin said. "Always losing things and later claiming somebody must've robbed 'em."

"Sure. You figured she wouldn't remember where she'd parted with that pin. But she wasn't that far gone when she came in here. She remembers she still had it on when she went into that room."

"She *thinks* she remembers."

"The cab driver that brought her here last night remembers too. He saw that pin on her when she got out of the cab."

He called my bluff: "She didn't come by cab. She was walking. Staggering."

I'd known Turpin to bluff too. I chanced it. "His hack number's 14-H32. His name's Joseph Morelli and he lives at 4007 North-West Pine Street and he has a girl just graduating from second grade."

It worked. "You've been busy," Turpin muttered. "Well, so what? So she was wearing this daisy pin when she come in here. Then she drank herself out of this world. Anybody could've gone in her room and lifted it off her."

"Uh-huh. Anybody named Turpin with a set of keys for all the rooms."

Turpin took the dead cigar from his mouth, looked at it with distaste, tossed it at the wastebasket. He heaved himself up out of the easy chair. "I think," he whispered, "I'll bust open that shoulder of yours again."

I stood up fast, spreading my feet a bit so I'd be able to move quickly. My insides felt too tight. I'd seen Turpin in brawls in the past. And I'd seen what the men he'd fought had looked like when he got through with them.

"The pin's only worth three thousand," I told him quietly. "That's legitimate retail, selling it out of a plush shop with a lot of overhead. For you it's hot, and it'll need time to cool off. You'll be lucky to get two hundred bucks for it from a fence.''

He started coming at me.

"Don't be a dope," I growled. "Two hundred's not enough profit for the chance you're taking.''

It stopped him. He looked at me, considering it.

"You're lucky the girl came to me first," I told him. "If I don't turn up that pin, she'll go to the law. The cops and the insurance boys won't take long in putting it on you the way I did. You're getting too old to enjoy that prison food.''

He leered at me. "I ain't so old yet. I always wondered if I could take you bare hands. What do you think?''

"I'm not in the mood right now. You need to let off steam, go knock down a wall.''

He laughed. But then he cut the laugh short and shook his head stubbornly. "You still're calling me a crook.''

I saw he was ready to get off the hook if I could give him a way to get off without losing face. I gave it to him: "Okay. You're not a crook. You're a private detective, and I'm asking you for some professional help. Somebody lifted the girl's valuable pin while she was sleeping it off in her room here. Suppose you try to locate whoever did it and persuade him to mail that pin to me. As soon as it comes to me, I'll send you your fee. A hundred bucks. And no strings attached.''

Turpin's burly shoulders relaxed a little. He rubbed his knuckles thoughtfully against the side of his florid nose. I didn't add that the hundred dollars, plus the cash he'd stolen from Diana Pines' purse, was almost as much as he could get for the pin by fencing it—and with no risk for him. We both knew that.

"Sounds pretty good," Turpin admitted finally.

"I thought it would. I'll just leave the job in your hands now. Till Monday." I turned and went to his door.

When I opened the door and stepped out, I almost bumped into a man in the corridor. He was a tall, well-dressed, darkly handsome man in his forties. There was a short, wide scar under his left eye, and the recently barbered hair showing below the brim of his hat was black with gray in it.

He smiled apologetically and murmured, "Pardon me." He walked around me and went on up the corridor and turned out of sight around a corner.

I looked at Turpin, standing just inside the doorway of his room. "Know him?" I asked.

Turpin glanced in the direction the man had gone and shook his head. "No. Why should I?"

"No reason. See you around." I went down the corridor and used the stairs beside the elevators. Down in the lobby, I bought a paper at the newsstand and settled down behind it in a chair partially screened by a limp potted palm.

I didn't have long to wait. The darkly handsome man I'd bumped into in the corridor—the one who could have been listening at Turpin's door—came down the stairs into the lobby. He crossed it without looking my way, went out the entrance. I left the newspaper behind and tailed him.

He walked to the downtown shopping area a few blocks away. Not once did he glance back to see if he was being tailed. I strolled just half a block behind him, beginning to think I'd been wrong.

Then a man, hurrying up from behind me, suddenly lurched sideways as he passed me. He bumped into me and grabbed hold of my arm for support, stopping me. He was a short, skinny man with a narrow face. His nose was crooked, the tip of it bent to one side. "Sorry," he mumbled, still hanging on to me.

I jerked my arm from his grasp, shot him a quick, suspicious look. He was either drunk or . . .

But then he stepped away from me, and I saw he limped. It was a bad limp, and he wasn't faking it.

"S'all right," I muttered, and hurried around him—just in time to see the man I'd been trailing abruptly turn into a big department store.

I was inside after him moments later, but he'd already merged into the Saturday shopping crowd. I prowled around the store for fifteen minutes trying to pick him up again and couldn't. It could have been that he'd known I was following him and done a fast and clever job of shaking me. Or he could have just lost me without intending to. Anyway, I'd lost him.

I used up two hours and eleven bucks in a nickel-and-dime stud game in the basement of the Central Tavern near the Dade County Courthouse. It was four thirty when I re-entered my office. Diana Pines showed up fifteen minutes later. I told her I expected to have her pin within the next couple of days and that I'd phone her when I got it. I said it with enough conviction to satisfy her. The delay didn't seem to worry her much. When she left my office I locked up for the day and went with her. She had a silver Mercedes-Benz parked outside. I waited while she climbed in and pulled away from the curb. Then I got into my Olds and followed her. I'd already botched one tail job that day, and it still smarted. I didn't botch this one.

The high brick wall set back from the road was crumbling and overgrown with thick, unkempt weed vines. The heavy iron gate at the driveway entrance through which the Mercedes-Benz had vanished was rusted and hung back on one hinge. From what I could make out in the moon-bathed darkness inside, the wall enclosed a small estate that had long ago been abandoned to decay.

Parking off the road under the wall, I switched off my headlights and motor and sat there for a moment, wondering what business Diana Pines could have in a seemingly empty ghost estate. Up till then she'd done nothing to justify my spying on her. She'd spent the afternoon shopping in several of the city's better clothing shops, had dinner alone in a restaurant that catered mostly to the expense-account crowd, and made a phone call. It had been night when she'd driven south to a section of Coconut Grove where the fine old houses were giving way to low-priced development cottages which in turn were giving way to shack slums.

I got the pencil-size flashlight from my glove compartment and walked from my car past the open and broken gate into the estate. Inside, its appearance of being a place long uninhabited increased. What had once been a small, well-ordered park was now a wild tangle of jungle. Stretching out on either side of the graveled driveway was what had once been lawn. It was now several acres of high weeds. In the deathly stillness, my shoes made too much noise on the gravel. I moved off it and pushed through the weeds toward higher ground where a building, or group of buildings, made a massive dark shape in the night. No light showed anywhere.

I found a path of broken flagstones and followed it. A sudden sound in the high weeds to my right made me jerk around, tensing. A big woods rat skittered across the flagstones and dashed into the weeds on the other side of the path. I let my breath out slowly.

My nerves were on edge. Continuing along the path I came to a row of hedges, shapeless and high as trees, and squeezed between them. Probably they had once formed a neat wall enclosing a tile patio and swimming pool. Weeds forced their way up between the patio tiles. The swimming pool was empty except for dirty puddles left from the last rain. The concrete of its walls and bottom was cracked and crumbling, covered in places by large patches of slimy moss.

Circling the pool, I pushed through the wild hedges on the other side and found myself looking up a weed-choked incline at a hulking, three-story French château large enough to contain about twenty-five rooms. Many of the slate tiles were missing from its peaked roof, the center portion of which was sagging badly. Several of the many slim brick chimneys were down. Most of the windows were shattered, and none of them showed anything but impenetrable blackness inside the mansion.

I waited for a few moments, looking around and listening. There was no sign of Diana Pines or her car—no sound from any direction. I moved up the incline to dispel the irrational feeling that the whole place was closing in around me. The huge, ornately carved, weather-ruined entrance door had a heavy chain spiked across it. I moved along the front of the building, past broken windows till I came to one that had no shards of glass in its lower sash. Hooking a leg over the window ledge, I climbed into the darkness inside the mansion—into the smells of decaying timbers and moldering furnishings and disintegrating plaster.

For the first few seconds I remained still, listening. Hearing nothing, I snapped on the pencil light and flashed its thin yellowish beam around. I was in a vast drawing room that had been furnished long ago by someone with a taste for outsized, ungainly imported European antiques. A faded and torn tapestry covered the wall to my left. On my right there was a fireplace big enough to drive a truck into. Against the far wall, on a dais flanked by long refectory tables, stood a gigantic carved-oak chair with a back fifteen feet high topped by a carved canopy. The center of the room was dominated by a massive octagonal table surrounded by chairs. Above it, from the twenty-five-foot-high ceiling, hung an elaborate chandelier, with snakes of dust-choked cobwebs dangling from its crystal pendants.

A thick mantle of dust covered everything in the room, and cobwebs were everywhere. An Oriental rug that almost managed to reach from wall to wall was badly decaying, in spots so badly that the timber of the floor showed through. There were several high doorways leading out of the room. I chose one of them at random and began wandering through the ruined, dark, silent interior of the mansion. Dust muffled my footsteps; the tiny beam of my pencil flashlight lighted the way for me. I wandered through a long, narrow passageway with standing iron candelabra, past walls on which hung pictures with the paint shredding off their canvases and the gilt peeling from their frames; through a living room dominated by a great organ that filled one wall; a sitting-room salon walled with antique mirrors; a game room with elephant tusks flanking each doorway and the mounted heads of wild Canadian and African animals hanging on the walls and lying about the floor where they'd fallen; a long, narrow dining room with an inlaid Moroccan tile floor and Italian Renaissance furniture.

Everywhere it was the same: the dust, the cobwebs, the darkness, the odor of decay and mold, and the thick, dead silence.

I found a narrow, curving stairway which led up to the second floor. I climbed it to a short hallway, entered a cluttered, overfurnished bedroom dominated by an outsize bed. The canopy that had once hung over the bed lay around it on the floor, its supports stood stark and bare.

I was about to turn away when I realized I'd seen something strange. Strange for that house, that is. Directing the narrow beam of my pencil light back to the bed, I moved closer to it. There was no cover on the bed. The sheets and the pillow were rumpled, darkly stained, discolored with age.

But there was no dust on them.

I was frowning at the bed when something else caught my eye. Light was coming through the bedroom windows.

I went around the bed to one of the windows and looked down through its cracked pane of glass. Behind the mansion was a stone cottage that must once have served as quarters for the servants. The light I'd seen was coming from the windows and open door of that cottage. A Cadillac convertible, a twelve-year-old model, was parked in front of the cottage. It was in need of a paint job, fender straightening, and a replacement for its patched canvas top.

Beside it, the moonlight shimmered against the sleek silver lines of the Mercedes-Benz.

Between the cars stood two women and a tall man. The light from the open doorway didn't quite reach the man and made it impossible to distinguish anything about him but his height. One of the women was Diana Pines. She had her back to the light, but I could make out enough of her to be sure.

The other woman was turned toward Diana Pines in such a way that the light from the doorway gave me a clear image of her. She looked about forty-five, had a tall drink in her hand, and was the same height as Diana Pines. The light glinted against the gray in her unkempt black hair. She must have been very pretty once, and she held herself as though she thought she still was.

"Wassa matter?" she was demanding loudly of Diana Pines. "It wouldn't hurt you t'stay awhile for once." Her voice was slurred and held the whine of the habitual self-pitier.

"I'm sorry," Diana Pines said, so softly I could barely hear her. "I've got to be getting home."

"Home!" the other woman growled, as if it were a nasty word. "You never stay any more. Just come and run."

"Stop it, Lorna," the man snapped at her. His head turned back to Diana Pines. "It's all right, Diana. I understand."

"Oh, sure," the woman he'd called Lorna grated. "I unnerstand, too. What the hell . . ." She shrugged melodramatically. "Anyway, thanks for bringin' the dough. Even if it isn't enough."

"It's the best I can do," Diana Pines said miserably. "You *know* that's the truth. I'd bring more if I could."

"Of course you would," the man said soothingly. "It's most generous of you."

Diana Pines looked from the man to the woman, her face masked from me by shadow. The man opened the door of the Mercedes-Benz for her, shut it after she climbed in behind the wheel.

"Drive carefully, Diana," the man said. "It was a pleasure having you visit with us again."

"A *rare* pleasure," the woman slurred. "An' a brief one."

Diana Pines turned on the headlights and motor. The man and woman stood aside and watched the Mercedes-Benz glide away.

As the sound of the car's engine died in the distance, the tall man turned savagely on the woman. "For God's sake, Lorna! When will you learn to shut up!"

"I can say anything I want to her!" the woman lashed back at him.

"The way you've been drinking, you don't know *what* you're saying half the time."

By way of answer, the woman raised her glass to her lips, tilted her head back flamboyantly, and drained her glass defiantly.

"You're going to get sick, really sick, if you keep that up," the man told her harshly.

"I'm not your patient, *Doctor*," the woman sneered. "Nobody is any more."

He slapped the glass out of her hand. It smashed against the gravel of the driveway.

"I hope," the woman told him viciously, "you ruin your lousy tires on that." She turned away from him and marched into the cottage. The man stood staring after her for a couple of seconds, then followed her inside, slamming the door shut behind him.

In the sudden silence, I was abruptly aware of the faint, whispering sound of footsteps sliding across the dust-covered floor behind me.

My mouth went dry. I spun around, swinging the pencil flashlight toward the sound. A man froze still at the end of its thin beam of yellowish light. He was tall, a head taller than me. He wore a soiled sweat shirt, faded dungarees, muddy white canvas tennis shoes, and he had the beautiful body of a Greek athlete's statue.

He blinked a couple of times at the beam of light, and then he came at me. He didn't look angry or upset. He was as purposeless and remorseless as an avalanche. I tried to slide away, but he was faster. A hand like a steel vise shot out and clamped around my wrist so tightly that my fingers sprang open. The tiny flashlight fell to the floor. I slugged the side of his head with my free fist and yelled to him to wait and talk it over.

But my punch didn't seem to hurt him, and I could see by his eyes that my words weren't registering.

I yelled at him again as loud as I could. His other hand, the one that wasn't busy crushing the bones of my wrist, clamped around my throat and shut off the yell abruptly. With my free hand I got hold of one of the fingers digging into my neck and tried to break it. I couldn't even bend it.

I kicked his shin hard with the point of my shoe. He grunted and shifted his feet a little, stepping on the little flashlight and crushing out the last shred of light in the room. Then both his hands were at my throat.

Desperately, swinging blindly in the total blackness, I punched him in the face, the belly, then the face again. I felt my knuckles thud against flesh and bone, but I might have been hitting stone for all the effect it had on him. He lifted me clear off the floor, bent me backward over the edge of the bed, began applying more pressure. I felt his thumbs sinking deeper, cutting off my air and blood. There was a roaring in my ears, and my eyes were bulging with the dammed-up pressure behind them. My own groping fingers finally found his eyes and dug in.

He didn't cry out. But his hands jerked away from my throat and he yanked himself backward into the darkness. I did a fast flip and roll across the expanse of the bed and came up on the floor on the other side of it, ready for him. He didn't come. He'd vanished.

I held myself perfectly still, gritting my teeth to quiet the sound of my hard breathing, waiting while my head shrank back to normal size. My eyes adjusted to the gloom and began to make out vague shapes by the faint moonlight filtering into the room. It didn't help. The room was too cluttered with outsize furniture which created darker shadows within shadows and made it difficult to distinguish substance from shadow. I strained my eyes, my ears. But there was no sign of him, not even the whisper of breathing.

Crouching down close to the floor, I waited for him to move, to show himself against one of the windows. After a few minutes my leg muscles began to cramp. With the discomfort came a feeling of foolishness. I'd done enough night fighting with the Rangers during the war to know the sharpness of my senses. No one could be in a room that size with me for that long without my detecting some sign of his presence. He could be anywhere else in that decaying mansion by then, ready to waylay me. But two could play at that.

Easing up off the floor a bit but keeping to a crouch, I drifted toward the doorway. I took it one step at a time, making no sound, and reached the door without seeing or hearing him.

His senses were sharper than mine. His fist exploded off the side of my jaw. The floor went out from under my feet. The wall crashed against my side and then tilted away, and the floor came up and slammed my back.

By the time my brain began to regain control of any part of me, he was kneeling on my chest and those steel fingers of his were sinking deep into my throat again. Weakly, I tried to fight him off me. My efforts were as ineffectual as those of a kitten caught in the jaws of a kill-trained Doberman.

Chapter 6

THERE WAS A BLINDING LIGHT SHINING IN MY EYES, AND the steel fingers were unlocking themselves from my tortured throat. After his weight left my chest, I realized I'd heard a man's voice saying something just before the hands released their death grip.

There were voices again, but the pounding of blood in my ears kept me from making out anything of what was being said except that two different men were doing the talking. After a while my head began to clear. The glare against my eyes shrank to the round yellowish eye of a normal-sized flashlight shining its beam at me. The guy I'd been tangling with had backed into the darkness beyond the small circle of light. I sat up slowly, laboriously, rubbing my bruised throat and gulping air through my open mouth.

"You're lucky I heard you yell," the man behind the flashlight said. "Sam might have killed you." It was the voice of the man I'd seen outside.

"Might've, hell!" I rasped. "He was going to."

"Of course. You had him worried. He saw you coming in through the gate and followed you here into the house. He couldn't understand what you were doing here. And then you turned on him and frightened him. So he attacked you."

"I frightened *him*?" I'd already been badly shaken. But the realization that he'd been right behind me from the moment I entered the estate without my knowing it shook me some more.

"Light some candles, Sam," the one behind the flashlight said.

There was the flare of a match. The flame touched the wicks of several candles in a standing candelabra beside the door. By their flickering light I saw the man holding the flashlight. He was also holding a small .25-caliber automatic pointed at me. And he was the same man who'd just been strangling me.

He was the same man—except that he looked older by about fifteen years and a bit heavier and softer and wearier. The same man—but he'd somehow changed to a light spring suit and black shoes. Also he was wearing glasses in front of his eyes and expression behind them.

Yet he was the same man. The same height, the same build, the same strong-featured handsome face—despite the difference of age and expression. I turned my head a little and looked at his other image, the one still wearing a sweat shirt, dungarees, tennis sneakers, and a total lack of expression.

The one with the flashlight and gun saw my puzzlement. "Sam is my twin," he said shortly, snapping off the flashlight and slipping it into his jacket pocket. He kept the tiny gun pointed at me.

I looked from one to the other. Sam looked as if he were only in his late thirties. The one with the gun was in his early fifties.

"All right," the one with the automatic snapped. "What are you doing here? Who are you?"

I continued to massage my neck with both hands, considering an answer to that.

"Speak up. Or would you rather I called the police?"

"Go ahead," I growled. "I was attacked for no reason by your brother here. With intent to kill. I'd like to talk to the police."

The older-looking twin frowned, suddenly uncertain of himself. "Sam and I live here. This is our home. You were trespassing."

"Yeah? How do I know this is your place?"

It kept him off balance and gave me time to think. His frown of uncertainty deepened. "Ask anyone in the neighborhood. I'm Doctor Boyd. Everyone knows that I . . ." Then he realized how I'd switched him to the defensive, and the lines around his mouth hardened. He lifted the little gun a bit to draw my attention back to its threat. "I asked you a question. I want an answer. What happens to you in the next few minutes depends on that answer."

"I was looking for 59 Manville Road," I told him. "Friends of mine live there. I'm expected at their house-warming party. I lost my way and came in here to ask directions."

While he was thinking that over, I put a hand against the wall and stood up. Sam started to take a step toward me, then hesitated and glanced at his twin.

But Dr. Boyd was concentrating on me. "I'm afraid," he said slowly, "that you are lying to me."

"Why? Haven't you ever gotten lost and had to stop somewhere to ask directions?"

"Why sneak into this building and go skulking around inside here? It's obvious no one lives here now."

I tried to think up an answer to that.

"So you see," Dr. Boyd said, "your story is most unlikely."

"All right," I told him reasonably. "I admit I was lying, about the last part. Not about the rest. I came in through the driveway to ask directions. Then I saw this abandoned mansion and curiosity got the better of me. I just came in for a look around. I couldn't know it belonged to anybody that'd care."

"Curiosity," said Dr. Boyd, "killed the cat."

"Now there's an original thought. Would you kindly put that gun away. It might go off."

"It might," Dr. Boyd agreed. "I believe you are still lying to me. We'll find out. If you are, it will be unfortunate for you. If you're not, I'll apologize for Sam having hurt you. Though you certainly can't blame him."

"You ought to keep him on a leash."

It didn't bother Sam at all. But it bothered Dr. Boyd. His face went stiff with anger. "Sam would never harm anyone unless he was provoked. As you provoked him. In that case he can be quite formidable as you've discovered. Nature's compensation to him, I suppose."

He didn't explain that. He didn't have to. I looked at Sam's expressionless statue-like face, and the answer was obvious. It was also obvious that Sam had received another compensation from nature. In his inability to think deeply enough to worry about anything too much, he'd found his own secret elixir of youth.

"Make sure he's not wearing a gun, Sam," Dr. Boyd ordered softly.

His twin blinked at him.

"A gun," Dr. Boyd repeated patiently. "See if he has a gun."

Sam nodded and drifted over to me. I held myself taut while he patted his hands over me. He shook his head at Dr. Boyd.

"Get his wallet and give it to me," Dr. Boyd told him.

Sam reached under my lapel for my wallet.

Taking one fast short sidestep that put Sam between me and Dr. Boyd's gun, I brought the hard heel of my shoe down on the top of Sam's instep. At exactly the right spot on the instep, there are a number of small, fragile bones. I felt some of them give under the sharp impact.

Even Sam couldn't take that. He gasped, yanked up his leg, and grabbed for where I'd hurt him. While he was balancing on one foot, I put both hands against his chest and shoved, getting all my weight and strength behind it. He flew backward and slammed into Dr. Boyd, who was trying to shift for a clear shot at me. They sprawled toward the floor together. Two running steps brought me beside them as they hit the floor. I brought my heel down hard on Dr. Boyd's right wrist, bent and snatched the tiny gun out of his sprung-open hand, and backed off fast.

Sam came up off the floor while Dr. Boyd was still struggling to a sitting position. He came limping after me.

I raised the gun. He saw it, but it didn't seem to mean anything to him. He kept limping toward me.

I backed away from him and yelled at Dr. Boyd, "Make him stop or I'll empty this into his stomach!"

"Stop it, Sam!" Dr. Boyd ordered sharply. "Come back here."

Sam halted, looked back at the twin who was so much older than he was.

Dr. Boyd stood up from the floor slowly. "Come back here," he repeated firmly.

Sam limped back to him.

"Now both of you move over there," I ordered, motioning with the gun. "Against that wall."

They obeyed, leaving the doorway clear. Sam leaned against the wall and raised his leg to hold his hurt foot with both hands.

"It will be all right, Sam," Dr. Boyd told him gently. "I'll take care of that as soon as this gentleman leaves."

I started cautiously across the room, moving so that I could keep my eyes and the gun on them the whole way.

"You may be sorry for this one of these days," Dr. Boyd murmured. "I have some friends . . ."

"That's hard to believe," I told him, and backed through the doorway out of that room.

I hurried through the building and got out the way I'd come in. At the foot of the incline below the mansion, I tossed the tiny automatic into the hedges and began running. It was hard to shake the feeling that Sam was running right behind me, soundlessly, about to reach out and get those hands of his around my throat again.

Chapter 7

I POURED MYSELF A DOUBLE BRANDY. THEN I MADE Kosterman his bourbon on the rocks and carried both drinks away from the little bony bar. We were in the gleaming stateroom of Kosterman's luxurious schooner yacht moored at the private dock of his estate. Kosterman sat deep in the leather sling of a big modern womblike chair. I handed him his drink, let myself sink into the twin of his chair, and took a healthy swallow of the brandy. I needed it.

"I appreciate this," Kosterman told me. "Your not barging right into the house. Diana'd be angry if she knew I'd hired you because of her. And she just now came home."

"I know. I was following her." It hadn't been easy to do. I'd been almost to Mayport, with the accelerator shoved down to the floor of my Olds, before I'd caught up to the silver Mercedes-Benz. I'd begun to think she'd lied about heading home when I finally sighted her car up ahead. After that I'd slowed and drifted back, just keeping her taillights in view till she pulled over the drawbridge onto The Island. I'd called Kosterman from the cop's guard hut; he'd suggested that we meet on the yacht and told the cop to let me through.

"You mean you actually did manage to locate Diana after I phoned you?" Kosterman asked, impressed.

I nodded, not explaining how easy it had been.

"Well, that's wonderful. Captain Crown was right to recommend you. Have you found out anything?"

"Do you know a man who calls himself Dr. Boyd?"

Kosterman's eyes became very unpleasant. "I know him." His thick, scarred fingers flexed slowly around his glass.

"*Is* he a doctor?"

"He was. Before he got disbarred—or whatever the medical profession calls it when they take away a doctor's license for unethical practices. Unethical—that's a business term for slimy."

"You know him pretty well."

His heavy shoulders shifted around under the expensive material of his sports jacket. Like many strong men who get too little exercise, he was addicted to small uses of his muscles to relieve tension. The harsh lines in his brooding face deepened. "He's married to my ex-wife," he said, pushing the words out slowly.

I had some more of the brandy while it sank in. "That'd be Lorna."

"Yes. You met Lorna?"

"Not exactly. Then Lorna Boyd is your daughter's mother?"

"Yes."

"That explains a good deal."

"What are you talking about?"

"Fill me in on the Boyds and your daughter."

He looked at me angrily. "That's a personal thing. And painful. And no concern of yours."

"Okay. You want me to find out what's troubling your daughter. You're paying me by the day. Put stumbling blocks in my way if you want. That way it'll take longer. And maybe I won't get anywhere. But if that's the way you want it . . ."

I let it hang there. Rudolph Kosterman rubbed a hand slowly back and forth over his knee, thinking it over. Finally he said, "Exactly what do you want to know?"

"I'm not sure. So you'd better tell me all of it."

He drew in a deep breath, let it out slow. He rolled his glass between his palms and brooded at the flames in the fireplace that made moving golden reflections against the rugged angles of his heavy face.

"I came up the hard way," he said slowly, talking to the fire. "No influential friends, no background, no money in the family. It's been a rough climb."

He stopped talking, lost in his thoughts. I nudged him. "You've come a long way, Mr. Kosterman."

"A long way," he agreed. "I started as a construction laborer. Unskilled. I never even went to high school. I've done a lot of reading in my old age to make up for that. But while I was fighting my way up, I was too busy just learning each job I took on. There wasn't any time for anything else."

His lips thinned, showing his teeth between them. "No time," he said viciously, "to add on that nice leisure-class veneer. . . . I was just an uncultured slob when I met Lorna. A *rich*, *successful* uncultured slob. Some of the things Lorna was born with rubbed off on me over the years. Manners, grammar, how to hold my fork. The *really* important things like that," he added with savage sarcasm. "It wasn't a very happy marriage. I divorced her ten years ago."

I waited, drinking some more of my brandy, relaxing as it took hold.

"I caught her cheating on me with Boyd," Kosterman went on finally. "It'd been going on a long time between those two. After the divorce she married him. I didn't have any trouble gaining full custody of Diana."

He drank some of his bourbon, and I watched him and waited, knowing none of this was easy for him.

Kosterman lowered his glass and wiped the back of his hand across his mouth. Remembering had set his face in lines of stolid anger. "Lorna's and Boyd's families were part of the same wealthy old-line circle. They've known each other since they were kids. I guess they'd have been married before I ever met her if things had stayed normal for them. But both their families lost everything in the crash. Boyd'd gone through medical school, as sort of a hobby I figure. So he could say he was something more'n just a rich nothing. But after the family dough went, he had to really work at it. He was making a decent enough living by most people's standards. But not by what he and Lorna were used to."

He started to take another drink, changed his mind, and forced himself to look directly at me. "Lorna was barely getting along on the charity of some distant relatives when I came along," he said flatly. "I was really impressed by her, by the background she represented. And I had enough dough to give her back the kind of life she'd lost. So she married me. But she never got over being ashamed of me. I guess Boyd was her escape valve. Well, she's got him for keeps now."

"When did Boyd lose his license to practice?"

"About five years ago. Seems he was bucking up his income by doing big-money abortions for girls that could afford it. One of the girls started bleeding after she got home. Her parents called in the family doctor, and she squealed on Boyd."

"What does he do now?"

Kosterman shrugged. "Nothing that I know of. I don't know how he manages to keep that place that belonged to his family going."

"He doesn't very well," I told him. "They're living in the servants' cottage."

Kosterman's vindictive smile told me something of how he'd gotten from an unskilled laborer to where he was. I'd've hated to be his personal or business enemy.

"They might as well," he said. "The servants are all gone. The only one left to do any of the chores around that place is that twin brother of Boyd's that never grew up in his head."

I nodded. "Sam."

"You were there tonight?"

"Following your daughter."

"Did she give them money?"

"I think so."

"I know so," Kosterman stated. "Diana's been sneaking money to her mother for years. She thinks I don't know about it, but I do. That's why I make sure she doesn't have much to give Lorna. Just her allowance." He smiled that savagely vindictive smile of his again. "I wouldn't be surprised if that's all Boyd and Lorna have had to live on for the past five years. Part of Diana's allowance. Though it's hardly enough to pay the taxes on that place of Boyd's."

"How long has your daughter been married?"

"Two years. Why?"

"You still give her an allowance?"

"Of course. I don't pay Darrell that much. He's still learning the business."

"Nice way to learn a business," I commented. "As the company's vice-president."

"Darrell's a good boy. A few more years and he'll be worth his position. He's had a rough time of it, that boy. He was a navy flier during the Korea thing. Got shot down and wounded. Escaped from a prisoner-of-war camp and won the Silver Star. But he's very modest about it. About everything. Sometimes I think he feels he hasn't earned his position in the company. But that's nonsense of course. Just because I had to work my way up from the bottom doesn't mean he should. What's the good of getting where I've gotten if I can't help the few people I care for?"

"About your ex-wife," I said, bringing him back to the point that interested me. "You think your daughter's been passing on some of her allowance to the Boyds regularly?"

"I'm sure of it. Diana and I are very close. She knows the divorce was Lorna's fault. She knows what Lorna did to cause it. But Diana can't help still having some feeling for her mother. Naturally she doesn't like the fact that Lorna's living in poverty now. For a cultured, beautiful woman like Lorna it's especially hard."

I remembered Lorna. "How long has it been since you last saw your ex-wife?"

"Ten years. Since the divorce. I don't want anything to do with that high-class bitch. . . . At first, after Boyd lost his doctor's license, Diana tried to persuade me to help them out. Can you imagine that? I wouldn't give those two the sweat off the back of my neck. . . . So Diana's been slipping them some of her allowance on the sly for years.''

''It doesn't bother you?''

Kosterman shrugged his heavy shoulders. ''It makes Diana feel better.''

I gazed into my glass for a moment, then looked up at Kosterman. ''You've been wondering what's troubling your daughter. Seems to me this situation with her mother would trouble any sensitive girl.''

Kosterman stared at me with a hard, calculating expression. ''That's your verdict? Lorna's what's bothering Diana?''

''Whatever it is could stem from that, yes.''

''You're way off the beam,'' Kosterman growled at me. ''Way off. This thing with Lorna's been going on for years. That wouldn't make Diana suddenly run out on her party the way she did the other night and go off on a bat in the city. She's never done anything like that before. So it's something new that's biting at her. And you've been wasting your time on the wrong things. Your time and my money.''

I stood up. ''You've already sent me the check to cover three days. I've only worked one day for you. Today. I'll mail your refund.''

''Don't be so goddamn touchy,'' Kosterman snapped. ''I know you haven't had enough time to work on it yet. I don't expect miracles. I'm just very concerned and too edgy because of it. Let it go at that.''

''You want me to keep on it?''

''When I fire you you won't be in doubt about it. I'm not subtle.''

I finished off the brandy and told him I'd be seeing him.

''Where're you going now?'' he demanded.

''Home. It's late.'' I left him there sunk in his womb-chair, sipping at his bourbon and brooding.

As I opened the louvered door of the stateroom, I caught the sounds of high heels clicking swiftly up the steps at the other end of the companionway that led between the two big guest cabins. I went through the companionway and up into the saloon. Rita Kosterman was there, over near the dining alcove. She had her back to me, facing a dartboard, three feathered darts in her hands.

As I came up into the saloon, she threw one of the darts. It missed the board completely and thudded into the teak wall beside it.

"You won't win any contests that way," I said.

She turned quickly, expressing surprise at the sight of me. She looked even cuter than I'd remembered—tiny and curvy in pale rose slacks and cardigan that set off the vivid blue of her eyes and the honey color of her hair.

"Oh!" she said as I came past the table toward her. "You startled me."

"I figured that," I told her. "How much did you hear?"

Rita Kosterman dropped her pretense and met my eyes thoughtfully. "Most of it," she said finally. "I followed Rudy from the house and eavesdropped deliberately."

"Why?"

"I was curious. And concerned. Tell me, is it ethical for you to be working for two clients at cross purposes?"

"I'm not sure of the cross-purposes part," I told her. "And I haven't taken any money from your stepdaughter yet."

She gave me a worried frown. "Does that mean you're not going to? That you won't find the pin for Diana?"

"I expect to have it back to her in a couple of days."

"Oh," she said, relieved. "That's wonderful. I should tell you I'm the one who suggested that Diana go to you— and not worry her father about it."

"I know. Why were you listening at the other side of the door?"

"I'm as concerned about Diana as Rudy is. He's right about something troubling her. I want to know what it is."

"You seem to be pretty good friends with your step-daughter. Tried asking her?"

Rita Kosterman nodded. "We are. And I have. She usually has a lot of respect for my judgment. I've been around and I guess it shows. But she won't tell me anything this time. Which makes me that much more worried.''

I said "uh-huh" meaninglessly, and took one of the darts from her hand. "I haven't tried this since I was a kid." I took careful aim at the dartboard and hurled it. The dart went wide of the center, but at least it hit the board.

Rita Kosterman grinned. "Amateur.''

"You didn't do so well yourself.''

"I knew you were coming after me. It made me nervous. Here . . .'' She turned a little away from me, sighted at the board, and tossed the last dart. Its metal point sank solidly into the bulls-eye.

"You've been practicing," I said.

"Uh-huh." She faced me again, and the bantering was gone. She'd made up her mind about something.

"Mr. Rome," she said seriously, "I don't know what kind of man you are or anything. But I'm asking you a favor. If you find out what's bothering Diana, please use some judgment about what you tell my husband. I could make it worth your while if that's the way you want it. It might be something Rudy shouldn't be told about.''

"Like what?''

She sighed and shook her head helplessly. "I don't know. It might be some personal problem that Diana just has to work out for herself. Rudy has a lot of faith in his ability to solve any problem that comes up. But in some cases he might just upset Diana more if he interferes.''

"I'll use my judgment," I promised her. "I usually do. It's lost me some clients.''

"I said I'd make it up to you," Rita Kosterman pointed out.

I shook my head. "That'd give me three clients at cross purposes." I studied her for a moment. "You know the trouble could still be what I told your husband—this business with her mother, Lorna Boyd.''

"No. I agree with Rudy on that. That situation's been going on a long time with no change.''

"It could have been building up in your stepdaughter,''

I said. "Over the years. She was only a kid when they got divorced. She's older now and a lot more aware of what's going on. It must be getting pretty deep under her skin . . . her mother having to live like that."

Rita Kosterman nodded, her eyes troubled. "I know. But there's nothing that can be done about it."

"Your husband doesn't strike me as the kind of man that takes kindly to advice. But my advice would be for him to settle an allowance on Lorna Boyd and her husband. Just enough so they can live normally. If he cares as much for his daughter as he claims to, it'd make her feel a lot better."

"Yes, it would. *I've* tried to tell Rudy that. But he won't. He never will. He hates those two."

"Ten years is a long time to hold that much of a hate."

"Don't get Rudy wrong, Mr. Rome. He's a damn nice man. But when he figures somebody's betrayed him, he doesn't forget it. And Lorna betrayed him worse than anybody ever did. He looked up to her too much, you see? Had too much respect for her background."

"How about you?" I asked her. "Does he respect your background, too?"

Her face darkened. "You're pretty smart, mister. Got me pegged and neatly pigeonholed already, haven't you? Well, you're right. I don't have any background worth mentioning. Or that I'd want to mention. And Rudy never cared enough to ask me. I guess Lorna soured him for good on the background bit."

"How'd you happen to meet him?"

She frowned at me. "You get real personal right off, don't you?"

"Nothing says you have to tell me . . . if you've got any reason not to."

Rita Kosterman considered that and shrugged. "We met four years ago in New York. Rudy was there on business and lonely. He picked me up. It was a pretty elegant bar, and Rudy was very polite about it. But that's what it was— a pickup."

"Worked out pretty well for you."

"Yes, it did. But don't make any mistake about that either. I've been a damn good wife to Rudy."

"He been a good husband for you?"

I was expecting her to get sore, but she didn't. She met my eyes unflinchingly. "The best," she said firmly. "Rudy's a lot like my father was . . . rough, honest, decent. Money hasn't changed him any. I'd bet he's no different than he was when he was a construction worker."

"Then you've got yourself a pretty unique husband, Mrs. Kosterman. There aren't many self-made men you could say that about."

"You're damn right. Any more personal questions?"

I started to turn away from her, then switched back and threw it at her: "What makes that daisy pin so important?"

"Huh?" She was thinking about something else, and it took her a moment to react. "The pin? Nothing, except that it's Diana's, and she wants it back of course."

"People don't go to a private detective to get their missing property back. They call the cops or their insurance company."

"I thought Diana explained it to you. Rudy's upset enough. We don't want to upset him any more."

"For a man with his dough, the loss of a three-thousand-dollar pin shouldn't be very upsetting. Especially if it's insured."

"It's not the money. It's the idea of her losing it—and how she lost it. It was a present to her. Rudy likes to give jewelry as presents. Both Diana and I have a lot of jewelry he's given us. For him it's the most romantic, sentimental. . . . Oh, hell! If you don't understand I can't explain it to you."

"I understand," I told her quietly. "What I don't understand is why two men busted into my boat and office and tore up both places searching for that pin."

"What?" She stared at me. "What two men?"

"I wish I knew."

She shook her head slowly, puzzled. "I don't under-

stand. You say two men you don't know searched your
boat and your office . . . for Diana's pin?''

"Uh-huh."

"Are you sure it was the *pin* they were looking for?''

"No," I admitted. "I can't be certain of that."

"Well, there you are! The kind of business you're in,
couldn't it have been something else they were hunting
for?''

"Could've."

"That must be it. Because Diana and I are the only ones
who know she lost the pin."

"And whoever stole it," I pointed out.

She shook her head again. "I'm afraid this is getting a
little too deep for me."

"That makes us even," I told her.

She sighed and looked across the saloon toward the
steps. "Rudy's probably in a black mood by now. I'd better go and kid him out of it."

I watched her cross the deck. When she was gone, I left
the yacht. My Olds was parked in the driveway in front of
the six-car garage. There was a white Jaguar convertible
parked beside it that hadn't been there when I'd arrived. I
was opening the door of my car when a voice sounded
behind me.

"I thought that was your car. I waited to see."

As I turned around, Darrell Pines came out of the darkness toward me.

He stopped a couple of feet in front of me, standing
stiffly erect, his hands shoved deep in his pockets, staring
at me coldly. "So Rudy decided to hire you after all."

Knowing about the Silver Star and how he'd earned it
made me feel more kindly toward him. "Rudy and I were
talking over old times," I told him. "Turns out he knew
my father."

"I don't like to be kidded," he warned me softly.

"You're a serious guy. I can see that. Just getting home
from the office?"

He started to say yes, then stopped himself and frowned

at me. "Rudy's paying you to find out why Diana walked out on the party and went on a tear. Right?"

"Ask him."

"Don't get wise with me, Rome. The kind of mood I'm in, I'm just itching to tangle with somebody."

"No thanks," I told him. "I've had mine for today."

It didn't mean anything to him. "Listen, what's Rudy paying you? I'll pay you the same. A little more if I can."

"To do what?"

"Nothing. To just forget it."

"Why?"

He grimaced, fighting a small war with himself. "What's biting Diana is nobody's business but hers and mine."

"If you know what's bothering your wife, you're the only one who does. What is it?"

"I told you, it's none of your business. Or anybody else's. And if you go finding out and tell Rudy, it'll only make things worse."

"Why don't you tell me and let me decide on that for myself."

Darrell Pines shook his head. "No. I don't know you enough to trust you that much."

"Well, that's that then." I slid in behind the wheel of the Olds and shut the door.

"Wait a minute!" Pines growled at me through the open side window. "Where're you going?"

"Home. Mind?"

"I made you an offer, dammit!" he said through his teeth.

"I'm up to my hips in offers today."

"What's that mean?" he demanded.

"Offer declined. Kosterman's my client."

He banged his fist softly against the side of my car door, trying to work off steam without hitting me. "Listen, Rome. . . ." There was suddenly a faint edge of pleading in his voice. It didn't come easy to him, and I didn't like having pushed him to it. He said, "Problems come up between husbands and wives. It happens all the time. And they usually work it out themselves if they're left alone to do it. Can't you leave it at that?''

Ordinarily, I'd have been inclined to do just that. But there was the strange matter of those two characters who'd chloroformed me. "We'll see," I told Pines.

"What's that mean?"

"What I said. We'll see."

Frowning uncertainly, he watched me shift into gear and drive away.

I came into Miami along Biscayne Boulevard, intending to keep going through to Dinner Key. But as I passed the dark city dock area, it reminded me of the two men who'd been waiting for me on the pier the night before. Cutting right on Northeast First, I drove toward the Miller Building to get my revolver from my office.

The building was pretty much deserted after noon on Saturdays. After six, it was locked up till Monday. I used my building key to get in the front door and took the self-service elevator up to the fifth floor. The door to my reception room was unlocked, the way I usually left it. I turned the knob and went in and flicked on the wall switch.

Ralph Turpin lay waiting for me on the floor of my office. A bullet had smashed against his forehead with the force required to break through the bone and destroy the brain inside.

I took one slow, shaky step deeper into the room and stared down at him. . . .

Chapter 8

FOR PERHAPS TWO MINUTES I JUST STOOD THERE GAZING down at him, seeking answers in the events of the thirty hours that had elapsed since he'd phoned me on the *Straight Pass*.

There were answers there, but they wouldn't come to the surface. I needed bait to bring them up. It was like when you go out in the Gulf Stream to fish and see a lot of sea hawks circling low over the water: those hovering birds tell you there have to be fish around there. So you cruise along slowly, trailing a hooked bait behind your boat. A big fish hears the sound of your engines and sees your wake and comes up out of curiosity to see what you're all about. And when he's up in your wake, he spots the bait and grabs.

I was like that boat, and those two characters with the sponge told me I'd already been leaving a wake. What I still needed was the right bait. I thought I knew what it was: a gold-and-diamond pin in the shape of a daisy. But I didn't have it. Not yet . . .

I went down on one knee and felt Turpin. His facial muscles were hard as stone. His arms and hands and torso were rigid. I took hold of the toe of his shoe and moved it back and forth. *Rigor mortis* hadn't progressed all the way down the legs yet.

The weather was mild. Not hot, not cold. So complete *rigor mortis* would occur in a minimum of about ten hours.

It hadn't gotten to all of Turpin yet. But it was getting there.

It had been five P.M. when I'd left my office with Diana Pines. It was now a little after one A.M. Eight hours. Which, judging by the condition of Turpin's corpse, was the minimum amount of time he'd been dead. Turpin must have come here and taken that bullet within minutes after I'd left.

Using my handkerchief, I picked up his .45 and examined it. One bullet had been fired from the clip.

I put down the gun and stood up, looked around. There was no bullet mark on the walls, floor, or ceiling. But I found something else on the floor of the corridor just outside the door to my reception room—a dried smear of blood.

I studied the far wall of the corridor. There was no bullet hole anywhere. I went slowly back along the corridor without finding any more blood. In the elevator I squatted over a dark stain the size of my hand on the floor. It was a bloodstain.

The killer had taken a bullet from Turpin's gun. A .45 delivers a terrible impact at close quarters. If the slug had hit the killer in something like the fleshy part of an arm or leg, it would have torn clear through and out. It hadn't. Wherever the killer was by now, he was in very bad shape.

I went back to my reception room, knelt beside Turpin, and went through his pockets without finding the daisy pin. Unlocking the inner door, I entered my office. Nothing there had been disturbed. I got the .38 Police Special in its clip-on holster from the middle drawer of my desk, fastened it to my belt under my jacket. Then I left the office, relocking the door.

I got Turpin's keys from his pocket and switched off the reception room light, then went out to my car. The weather was still mild. But the back of my shirt was drenched.

I had to fight the urgency that nagged at me all the way to break the city speed laws. Parking a block from the Moonlite Hotel, I walked rapidly the rest of the way and entered the building via the service alley and the fire-escape door and got to the second-floor corridor without being seen.

It felt as if I'd spent an unwarranted amount of time fumbling with the keys before I found the one that unlocked Turpin's door. Inside, I relocked the door before switching on the light. Someone had been there before me. The room had been searched as completely, and with as little regard for concealing the search job, as had my boat and office. The searcher hadn't missed any of the likely hiding places. But I was willing to bet that he'd overlooked the right one. I had the advantage there. I knew about Turpin's favorite concealment gimmick.

I found a beer-can opener in the medicine closet and used it to take the bathroom door off its hinges. Placing the door across the bed, I squatted down and found what I'd been expecting. Turpin had used a knife to gouge a cavity inside the bottom of the door. The hole was just big enough for the pin. But there was nothing in it.

There had been.

A tiny piece of Scotch tape still stuck to the rough wood inside the hole. I peeled it off. The way it peeled and the way it looked told me it had been stuck in there fairly recently.

Getting the bathroom door back on its hinges, I used my handkerchief to wipe off all the smooth surfaces I'd touched. I was glancing around, making sure I hadn't overlooked anything, when a loud double knock sounded against the door of the bedroom.

I froze, staring at the door.

"Turpin?" It was Welch, the night manager of the Moonlite. "Turpin!"

In the corridor Welch would be able to see the thread of light under the room door. If he had a key to the room and used it, I was sunk. The combination of Turpin's corpse in my office and me in his searched room would finish me. I listened to the slow thudding of my heart.

"Turpin!" Welch shouted angrily. He pounded at the door.

I waited. For thirty seconds I worked at an ulcer. Then I moved to the door. Welch might be outside. Or he might have gone down to the lobby for the room key. I had to gamble.

I sucked in a deep breath, unlocked the door, yanked it open. Welch wasn't there.

Turning off the light, I stepped into the empty corridor, shut and locked the door from the outside. I made a fast thing of getting out the way I'd come in.

Turpin was still waiting for me in my reception room, exactly the way I'd left him. Wiping off the keys, I slipped them back in his pocket. I used my handkerchief to dry my face, neck, and hands, filled a paper cup with water from the cooler and gulped it down, filled it again, and drank that one more slowly.

Then I made my phone call to the homicide bureau.

Chapter 9

ART SANTINI'S HOMICIDE OFFICE WAS ONE OF SIX FORMED by subdividing what had been a wide outside corridor with gray metal partitions and doors. It was barely large enough to contain its desk, the three metal chairs, and the two tall filing cabinets which were the same gray as the walls and door. Its size and color, and the bars over the single window, gave the office the look of a jail cell.

"The papers probably have the story on the presses by now," Santini mused unhappily. "It'll be a beaut. Man's shot to death right in the heart of downtown, and we don't even find out about it till almost nine hours later. A beaut."

His remark didn't call for any comment from me. He was talking to himself and the walls as much as to me. Art Santini was a short, plump man with a wide, roundish face, a sharp nose, and a small, soft pink mouth. This face, and the expression of his dark, liquid eyes, gave him a look of gentle softness and puzzlement that was entirely misleading. We'd started on the force as rookies the same year. The name wedge on his desk had "Lieut. A. Santini" printed on it in black letters. I'd been the second man out of our group to make lieutenant; he'd been the first.

It was about five in the morning, and we'd been waiting an hour for a call from Captain Jones, Santini's boss in Homicide. We were both bleary-eyed as we finished off the containers of black coffee and the limp sandwiches he'd had sent over from The Owl, an all-night diner a couple of blocks away.

"The pressure for an arrest on this one's going to be something," Santini said. "That could make it rough on somebody."

"Meaning me?"

He sighed and nodded. "Could be, Tony."

"The department'll really have to be reaching," I said, "to tap me with this one."

"You've got no alibi for the time he was shot," Santini pointed out gently.

"No motive either. And no evidence. You knew Turpin, too. You liked him about as well as I did. How's *your* alibi?"

"It wasn't my office he was found dead in, Tony."

The phone on his desk rang. He picked it up, said "Yeah?" into it, listened, said "Yeah" again, and hung up. He put both hands on the desk and stood up. "Okay, Tony, let's go."

I got up as he opened his door. He looked at me and warned softly, "Watch your step with the captain."

I nodded and led the way down the narrow corridor and around the corner. The uniformed police secretary at the desk beside the captain's door told us to go in. The captain's office was like Santini's except that it was twice the size, and had more chairs and no bars on the windows. Captain Jones sat behind his desk, a tall, angular man in his fifties, with a lean, hard face and a long jaw. His mouth was tight and bitter, the eyes behind his horn-rimmed glasses sensitive, and his gray hair was crew cut to show the good strong shape of his skull. Petrov, from the district attorney's office, slumped in a chair beside the captain's desk. He was a stocky man with a squarish face and hyperthyroid eyes. He'd been yanked out of a sound sleep for this, and he looked determined to stay irritated about it.

Captain Jones jerked a thumb at one of the chairs in front of his desk. I sat on it. Santini closed the door and leaned against it, staring at the opposite wall with the look of a man dissociating himself from the unpleasantness.

Captain Jones kept looking at me. The light from his desk lamp glinted against his glasses, hiding the expression of his eyes. He shuffled together the papers on his desk and planted his palm on the pile like he was driving the last nail in my coffin. "What was Turpin doing in your place?" he began softly.

"I don't know. Lieutenant Santini had my statement typed up two hours ago. You've read it by now."

"You don't know," he repeated softly. "Was Turpin in the habit of dropping in at your office?"

"No."

"When was the last time he did?"

"It's been quite a while."

"Quite a while . . . Earlier the same day you visited Turpin in his room at the hotel. When was the last time you paid him any visits?"

"The same thing. Quite a while."

Jones nodded slowly. "What did you go to see him about?"

I got out a package of Luckies and lit one, puffed at it with what I hoped was passing for nonchalance. "I've got a client who's worried about his daughter's goings-on. Couple of nights ago she stopped at the Moonlite. I went over there to ask Turpin if she'd had anybody with her. He said she was alone."

Petrov hunched forward on his chair, his hyperthyroid eyes suspicious and eager. "This client got a name?"

"Rudolph Kosterman. Big businessman. Lives on The Island up in Mayport."

"That's out of our territory," Petrov muttered, still suspicious. "But we could always check that through the cops up there."

"You can check it easier than that. Try Captain Crown, right here. He recommended me to Kosterman for the job."

Petrov slumped back, disappointed.

Captain Jones said, "Tell me about your other clients."

"Haven't got any others at the moment."

Jones eyed me quietly for a moment, then leaned back and said, "The medical examiner's pegged the time of death between four thirty and five thirty P.M."

"I didn't leave my office till five," I told him. "That narrows it to between five and five thirty."

Petrov leaned forward again. "Unless," he pointed out, "the death occurred just *before* you left your office."

"Cut the comedy," I snapped, letting some of my own irritation come through. "You know damn well I didn't shoot Turpin."

Captain Jones asked softly, innocently, "*How* do we know you didn't?"

"Turpin shot whoever did it. You know that. I'm not tough enough to be walking around with a .45 slug in me and not show it. But I'll be glad to strip for you if you want to look."

"You could've had somebody else with you. This somebody else could be the one that took the bullet."

"I could've been there when Turpin got it," I agreed. "But I had no reason to want Turpin dead."

"Him and you used to be partners in that agency of yours. The rumor is you bought him out because you caught him trying to blackmail a client. There was bad blood between you when you split up."

"Sure. So I think it over for a whole year and then decide I'm mad enough at Turpin to kill him. I phoned him and invite him over to my office. Of course I make sure I've got somebody else with me, to witness my murder. I shoot Turpin, and Turpin shoots my witness. . . . By the way, how'd ballistics make out with the tests on my gun?"

"It didn't fire the .38 slug they took out of Turpin's head. But that doesn't mean anything. You could've used another gun for the job."

I blew some smoke across the desk at Captain Jones.

"Turpin's room'd been searched by somebody. Know why?" Captain Jones barked.

"No."

He passed that by. "According to the day clerk at the Moonlite, you were there to see Turpin around two thirty yesterday afternoon. Shortly after you left, Turpin went out. He came back about two hours later. Went up to his room. Came storming back down a minute later, looking sore as a boil about something, and went out again. That was around twenty to five, as far as the day clerk can remember. Figuring the distance to your office, and the time he died, it looks like he went straight from the Moonlite to your place. Any idea why?"

"I told you before. No." I told the lie straight faced.

"Let's try another one of my hilarious guesses," Jones said flatly. "Turpin got back to his room and found it'd been searched. He had a reason for thinking you might've been the one did the searching. He stormed over to your place to have it out with you. How's that sound?"

It sounded too close to what could actually have happened. I said, "I don't know any more about it than you do, Captain."

"Goddamnit! He was killed in your office!" Petrov shouted.

"I've got no idea why. Somebody could've followed him there and decided it was a good place to do the kill, with the rest of the building empty that time on Saturday."

"Who?" the captain demanded.

"How would I know? He had a lot of enemies."

"Name them."

"There's too many. I don't know anybody that had anything to do with Turpin that liked him. He was that kind of guy. It's been a year since I've known anything about what he was up to. He must've accumulated a lot more enemies in a year."

"We're checking on that," Captain Jones stated. "Rome, you do realize that your license depends on your co-operating with the police?"

"I realize it."

"Just reminding you. Because if I find out you're playing games with me on this case, I'll see to it your license is suspended. Permanently. That'll be the least of what happens to you."

I crushed out my cigarette in his ashtray and stood up. "I take it that means I can go now?"

Captain Jones nodded. "Don't make any trips for a while," he said in the same soft, even voice he'd used throughout the session. "I'll be wanting to talk to you again."

"Any time." I looked at Petrov. "Give my regards to the D.A."

"Listen, you cocky bastard," Petrov snapped, "don't act flip with me. You've been asking for it ever since you shot off your big mouth and got kicked off the force. I've got a hunch we're going to tie the can to you sometime."

"It's been tried," I told him. "By men who knew their jobs a lot better than you do."

"Cut it out," Captain Jones said. "Both of you. You can pick up your gun from the man outside, Rome."

I looked at Santini. He opened the door and stood aside. I went out and got my .38 from the police secretary and headed for the elevators.

Santini caught up with me as I stepped into the elevator. He rode down with me, saying nothing. When we got off on the ground floor, he waited till we were alone in the entrance lobby.

"I'm sorry they braced you like that," he told me sadly. "I know you didn't have anything to do with killing Turpin."

I said, "Thanks."

"But they're going to lean on you real hard, Tony. If you're holding back anything, it might be a good idea to tell me about it. For your own protection. You know I'll do my best to keep you out of trouble, whatever you tell me."

"I'm surprised at you, Art. I was on the force too long for this old alternating hard-and-soft routine to work on me. Jones and Petrov pound me, and then you cuddle me. You know better."

Santini actually blushed. "Okay. So I know better. But

I know something else, too. I'm damn sure you weren't being straight with the captain in there.''

"I'm not dumb enough to lie to him about a murder."

"Not lie," Santini said, eying me wisely. "But you could just leave out telling the captain some things you know. I think that's what you did. Tony, they'll really hang one on you if you interfere with us nailing Turpin's killer."

"I'm not likely to do that," I told him. "I've got my own reason for seeing to it Turpin's killer doesn't get away with it."

"What reason are you talking about?"

"I'd've been dead three years ago if Turpin hadn't squeezed a trigger at the right second. He didn't do it to save my guts. He did it for the bonus we were getting from the Truckers' Association for stopping the gang that'd been looting their sheds. And we didn't like each other any better after he did it. But still, he did do it. And I owe him something for that."

"Wherever Turpin is now, he couldn't care less any more."

"We both know where he is. And you couldn't be more wrong. Turpin was always a guy to hold a grudge. He'd enjoy having the one who killed him sent down to join him."

"Play your own game in this, Tony, and you could get into worse trouble than you're in now."

"Well," I said, "Turpin would enjoy that, too." I left him and went out to my car.

The sun was just rising over the white towers of the Miami Beach hotels across Biscayne Bay, tipping them with a rosy hue. The Sunday dawn spread across the water and flattened against the buildings of Miami City, turning them into a crazy patchwork of dark-shadowed sides and golden-glowing sides. Without people the buildings and streets took on the innocent, inorganic look of a mountain of various-sized blocks that had been kicked over by a bored kid and left scattered around in a haphazard jumble. It took people to give a city life. That morning it looked better to me without them.

At Dinner Key I unbuttoned my jacket and put a hand on the grip of my .38 before starting out on my pier.

But there was no one waiting for me on the *Straight Pass* except Tangerine. He was asleep in a tight ball on top of the fish box in the stern. I guess the smell of it gave him pleasant dreams. As I climbed down into the cockpit, he got up, arching his skinny back in a stretch that lengthened him by half. Then he followed me into the galley.

I put down some milk for him, poured myself a stiff brandy. Tangerine finished his breakfast and left. I downed my drink and went into the cabin, changed to pajamas, and stretched out on the bed. After five minutes, I sat up again, my eyes still wide open. This time reading seagoing history, usually my best relaxer, didn't help. I finished the last chapter of Coxere's *Adventures* still tense.

Finally, I got up and went back to the galley. I got the brandy bottle and carried it back to bed with me. After I'd had enough, I went to sleep. I dreamed that it was three years ago and I was back on the roof of the freight shed. I was down with that bullet in my smashed shoulder, waiting helplessly while that hood took his time aiming the gun at my face for the finishing shot. . . .

Chapter 10

ANNE ARCHER'S SPACIOUS HOTEL SUITE WAS DONE IN softly pleasing modern. The feeling of space was enhanced by the wide ceiling-high doorways and the way the living room flowed up two wide, low steps to the open dining level. The living room had dark-stained walnut walls and very pale pink carpeting and curtains on the floor-to-ceiling windows. There were a few sharp color accents—the polished bronze of a lamp base, the dark rose of one chair, the deep green of a sofa pillow.

It was seven o'clock that Sunday evening, and I was wearing my best dark-blue wash-'n'-wear suit and a knitted maroon tie. Anne Archer wore a form-hugging green cashmere sweater and skin-tight dark-blue slacks that emphasized the slinkiness of her tall, slender figure. I'd phoned her an hour earlier, and I was pleased by the notion that she'd dressed this way for me.

I watched her as she carried our drinks back from the tiny bar beside the hi-fi set in one corner of the living room. Her loose-flowing red hair and her sure, graceful walk added up to the same delightful effect I remembered from two nights before. She set the glasses on a long, low coffee table with ebony legs and a white marble top and perched on the edge of the pale pink sofa. I sat in the rose chair, which gave me the best view of her long, exquisitely curved legs, and picked up my brandy.

"I stocked the bottle of brandy especially for you," she said, tasting the Scotch and soda she'd made for herself.

"I had a hunch you'd be popping back into my life one of these days."

"I'm flattered."

"You should be. And I shouldn't be so obvious. I keep telling myself to play hard to get. I was going to, too. When you phoned I was hoping it was for a date tonight. So I could turn you down. I've got a date later. And I don't enjoy being asked the last minute."

"I tried getting in touch with you yesterday," I lied. "But you didn't answer your phone."

"Oh? Well, now it's my turn to feel flattered. When did you call?"

"Around five o'clock in the evening." I sipped the brandy and watched her carefully without appearing to.

She frowned, remembering back, then shook her head at me. "You couldn't have. I was here at five."

"It might've been a little before or after five. I wasn't keeping close tabs on the time."

She shook her head again. "I was shopping yesterday afternoon, but I know I was back here by four. I had to take a shower and get dressed for a date. And I didn't leave till six thirty, when my date showed up for me." She eyed me suspiciously. "Are you sure you phoned me yesterday?"

"Maybe while you were in the shower, " I said. "It's just as well I wasn't able to reach you. You sound as though you're booked solid. That man-woman ratio you were complaining about doesn't seem to cramp you much."

She turned her head and gazed solemnly out the huge window, past her small balcony at the surf pounding the beach. "I had the blues that night. . . . What's a woman supposed to do when she comes down here for a divorce? Sit by herself night after night for six straight months? I couldn't stand that. I don't like myself enough to do it. And I do like men . . . the ones who're attractive and interesting."

I drank down the rest of the brandy. "I guess Darrell

Pines scores on both accounts," I said lightly. "Attractive and interesting."

She was picking up her glass. She set it down again, stared at me. After a moment she asked quietly. "How do you know about that?"

"You forget. I'm a detective. A dirty line of work, remember? But it keeps me professionally attuned to the meanings behind what people do and say. I saw the way Pines and his wife acted toward each other when I brought her home. And you told me you felt it was your fault that she'd gone off on a binge. Two and two still adds up to four."

Her eyes narrowed.

"I wish now," she said fiercely, "I hadn't bought that bottle of brandy. Serves me right. Thinking you were interested in me."

"I am."

"No, you're not. And you're not so damn perceptive after all. I get it now. The light dawns. Diana told you. She hired you to find out how far it's gone between Darrell and me. Didn't she? Maybe even to make me stay away from Darrell from now on?"

I didn't say anything. I could see that she'd been wanting to tell it to somebody anyway.

"Well, you tell Diana she can stop worrying about it. What happened the night of the party never happened before. It was the one and only time. And it didn't mean a thing. Nothing."

"What did happen?"

Anne Archer grimaced angrily at me. "Stop playing me for a fool. You know, Diana must have told you. But it didn't mean what she thought it did."

She glared down at her clenched fists for a moment. When she spoke again, her voice was quieter, more controlled. "Diana knows how it's been for me since I left my husband. I've been doing the all-too-usual desperate divorcee bit. Trying too hard to prove to myself that I'm still attractive to men. I know I've been doing it. I don't like myself for it. But the night of that party I had a little too much to drink and did it again. Only this time with her husband. It never happened before."

She looked up at me, her face taut. "Disappointed?"

"No."

"I guess Diana will be. I know what she must think after catching Darrell and me in that clinch in the guest room. But that was the only time it ever happened. And it's not all my fault either. Darrell has his own problem. And I'll bet Diana is so wrapped up in herself she isn't even aware of it. Darrell isn't supposed to have any problems. After all, he's got the fair Diana and he's heir apparent to Rudy Kosterman's company. But lately he's gotten the feeling he's just a piece of property owned by Diana and her father. I know it bothers him a lot. Maybe it's time Diana knew it."

"Maybe it is," I agreed softly.

Anne Archer sighed and shook her head angrily. "No I know it's no excuse. Darrell and I both had too much to drink that night. That's all. We started flirting with each other. Just kidding, really. But somehow we ended up in that real convincing-looking clinch. And Diana had to walk in on us at that exact moment. . . . I couldn't feel worse about it. Even though it didn't mean anything really. I'll never forget how shocked Diana looked before she ran out. She's such a damn innocent kid. If it'll make her feel better about anything, I feel rotten about hurting her like that. It's made me realize what a bitch I've become. You can tell her that."

"You're mistaken," I said. "Your friend Diana didn't hire me to pump you for information."

That it was the truth helped me make it sound convincing. Anne Archer stared at me, uncertainly replacing her anger.

We were interrupted by the ringing of the phone on the table. She jumped up off the sofa and went across the room toward it.

I stared down at my empty glass. I'd found out what I'd come to find out. I'd already guessed it pretty accurately because of the way Darrell Pines had been so anxious to keep Kosterman from knowing.

By the bar, Anne Archer was snatching up the phone. "Yes?" She listened for a short time, then said, "I wouldn't know. I haven't seen anything of Nimmo in over a month. . . . No, I have no idea where he's living now. . . . Well, that's *his* problem. . . . That's all right."

She hung up the phone and turned slowly, looking across the room at me. "Are you still here?" she demanded without heat. "I've got a date to get dressed for now."

"I could use another drink," I told her.

"I'd rather you left now," she said flatly.

"I'm sorry you feel that way."

"You came here for a reason. To get information out of me—"

"One of these evenings we'll make it just for fun," I said. "If your waiting list shrinks a little."

I left her standing there with the unfinished drink in her hand, went to the door, and let myself out. I mulled over what she'd revealed as I rode down in the elevator and went out through the glass lobby door the uniformed doorman held open for me.

Anne Archer had told me what was troubling Diana Pines. And it fitted neatly enough.

The trouble was it didn't really tell me anything I hadn't already guessed. It didn't tell me why the search jobs had been done on my boat and office and on Turpin's hotel room—apparently for a decorative pin that wouldn't bring enough to be worth the trouble. It didn't tell me about the two men who'd chloroformed me or about the man I'd caught listening outside Turpin's door.

And it certainly didn't tell me why Turpin was dead.

I had a date of my own that evening in Key Largo. An old friend had sunk all his cash and credit into building a new motel down there and was throwing a party to celebrate its opening. The party lasted till the early hours, by which time I didn't feel up to driving. So I got my sleep in one of the motel cabins and drove back up to Miami in the morning.

It was ten thirty Monday morning when I got to my office. There was mail waiting for me in my reception room—letters, bills, advertising circulars, the check from Kosterman. And a package. I took the mail with me into my inner office and sat down behind my desk. Pushing the small pile of envelopes to one side, I set the package on top of the desk in front of me.

It was a small, flat package, wrapped in the kind of white paper available in most five-and-tens, tied with brown string that you could buy almost anywhere. My name and address had been printed on it in crude block letters, with a ballpoint pen. There was no return address. According to the post-office mark, the package had been mailed to me Saturday afternoon.

I broke the string and unwrapped the paper. Then I opened the small white box inside. There was nothing on or in the box that told me who'd sent it. I took out what was inside and held it in the palm of my hand, gazing at it.

It was a pin in the shape of a daisy, with gold petals and a cluster of diamonds forming the round center.

Chapter 11

It was on one of those North Miami Avenue blocks with a portico shading the sidewalk. The narrow store front was cramped between a Cuban bar and an open-air pool hall. The sign over the window, which was crammed with the usual conglomeration of poor people's treasures, read:

LOANS
FAST—CONFIDENTIAL
$5—$500
GUNS—DIAMONDS—CAMERAS

A cardboard sign over the door said: "Old-Rare COINS—Bought & Sold." The inside of the glass in the door was covered with small yellowing cards to which coins were pasted, with a description of each scribbled on its card.

A cowbell clanked as I opened the door and went in.

There was barely room for five people to squeeze into the space between the counter and the wall. There was a glass case containing old coins, cameras, and jewelry on either end of the counter, and rifles and handguns displayed on wall racks flanking the curtained doorway behind the counter. As the door swung shut behind me, the cowbell stopped clanking. Sands, the owner of the store, came out through the doorway curtain behind the counter.

He was a very tall, very skinny, completely bald man in his forties. He wore a black-leather bow tie, and his pipe-stem arms hung abnormally long from the short sleeves of his gaudy sports shirt. When he saw me, he put both hands flat on the counter and licked his thin lips while he tried to hide the jolt of terror that hit him. Then he forced a big smile, showing gold teeth and some missing ones.

"Well, well, Mr. Rome," he blurted with false cordiality. "Been a long time since I seen you last."

"Uh-huh," I said. "More than a year. Not since Turpin and I split up."

The terror flickered in his eyes again. He blinked rapidly.

Now I was sure I'd been right. Before it had just been guesswork. After I'd left Turpin's room the day before, he'd gone out and hadn't returned for about two hours. If he'd had the daisy pin in his room all along, it wouldn't have taken that long to go to a store, buy string and wrapping paper, package the pin, and drop it in a mailbox. I'd put that together with the fact that I knew Sands did some side fencing of small items of hot jewelry. And that Turpin had used him a couple of times back in the days when I sometimes knew what Turpin was up to.

"I guess you know what happened to Turpin," I said to Sands.

He started to reach up a hand to his bow tie and dropped it quickly back on the counter. But not quickly enough to hide its trembling. "Yeah," he said sorrowfully. "In the papers this morning. Lousy break. Who could've done a thing like that to old Turpin?"

"That's what the cops want to know. They want to know it real bad. They're looking for everybody that had anything to do with Turpin recently. Sweating each one till there isn't a single thing about any of them they don't find out."

Sands licked his lips again, stared at me with horrid fascination.

I took the daisy pin out of my pocket and placed it on the counter between his hands.

He looked down at it, then slowly up at me. He didn't say a word. His eyes looked close to tears.

"Turpin sold that to you," I said.

Sands cleared his throat. He whispered, "No."

"Yes. He did. Saturday morning. Saturday afternoon he came in again and bought it back from you. Same price. He gave you back your dough and took the pin and went out with it."

Sands tried to say something, couldn't, and shook his head instead.

"Open up," I told him, "or I'll feed you to the cops. This can bring you the worst trouble of your life. This rap isn't just fencing a few hot jewels from time to time . . . though that alone'll bring you more trouble than you can take. This is a murder, Sands. And this pin's part of the murder setup."

"I didn't!" Sands croaked. "He didn't sell this to me! I never bought it."

"You can tell me the truth," I said softly, "or I can bring the cops down on you. There's no other way. I'm in too deep myself to spare you any pity. Murder changes everything."

"I don't know anything about Turpin's murder," he pleaded.

"When it's a murder investigation," I said, "the boys can get pretty rough on even ordinary, honest citizens. With someone like me, they get even rougher. But somebody like you, Sands . . ." I punched his bony chest with the tip of a stiff forefinger. "With somebody like you, they take you down to the basement and all rules are off. They'll sweat blood out of you. You'll sweat till there isn't a drop in you they don't know about."

"I don't know who killed Turpin!"

"You know about this pin though."

"I didn't buy it from him. I swear it."

"Okay." I scooped the pin off the counter and turned away. "You want it this way—"

"Wait!"

I turned back to him.

"I told you the truth," Sands said weakly. "But not all of it. I mean . . . he came in here Saturday morning like you said. But I was too busy right then to give him time, and he was in a hurry. So he left this pin here with me. For me to figure out later how much I'd pay him for it. He said he'd be back."

"When'd he come back?"

Sands raised both trembling hands and shrugged. "I don't know exactly. I had to go out for a while Saturday afternoon. My wife's sick. In bed. I had to go home, make her something to eat, see how she was. I got back here around four. Turpin was waiting for me outside."

"He wanted the pin back?" I asked.

Sands nodded. "But first he wanted to know how much it was worth. When I told him it wasn't worth anything, he took it back and went away, and that's all I know. I swear it."

I opened my hand and gazed at the daisy pin, raised my eyes to his. "Come again. About its not being worth anything."

He blinked at me, not understanding the look on my face. "I appraised it later Saturday morning, a couple of hours after Turpin brought it in. When I got a couple minutes free. It's a phony. I told Turpin that when he came back."

"These gold petals? The diamonds?"

"The gold's real enough. The diamonds ain't. And there ain't enough gold on that thing to make it worth more'n twenty bucks, retail. Not worth a nickel, to me."

"You're sure of this."

Sands was insulted. "Of course I'm sure."

I nodded, dropped the phony pin in my pocket, and left. I stopped off at my bank and deposited Kosterman's check. Even after drawing out enough money to maneuver on, it left enough to start thinking about the horses running at Hialeah. But there was no time for going out to the track, or even for doping one race and phoning a wager to my bookie. I headed back to my office. Margo, in Ben Silver's office next door, had a message for me. Diana Pines had called from The Island and wanted me to phone her back.

In my office I sat behind my desk, placed the daisy pin

on the desktop in front of me, and stared at it for a few minutes. It winked at me, reflecting the sunlight streaming in through the windows behind me.

Real, it wouldn't have been worth enough to cause all that had been happening around me in the past few days.

But if it was worthless . . .

Then it *might*.

I put through the call to Diana Pines.

"Have you got it yet?" was the first thing she said when she came on the phone. "My pin?"

"Almost," I told her.

"Almost? What in the world does that mean?"

"I'm not sure myself."

"Sounds to me," she said angrily, "like you're giving me the old run-around. I'm tempted to just tell my father I lost the pin and get it off my chest."

"Good idea," I told her. "Why don't you?"

"I was going to. But Rita still doesn't think it's a good idea."

Suddenly, Rita Kosterman's voice came through the connection. "That's right. I don't."

"Rita!" Diana Pines blurted. "I didn't know you were—"

"I just picked up the extension in my room to make a call," Rita told her. Then she said to me: "Mr. Rome, it's not your business to give us personal advice. You're supposed to be finding that pin. Do you mean to say you haven't managed to locate it yet?"

Instead of answering, I asked, "Was a copy ever made of any of your jewelry? That pin in particular?"

"No." Diana said. "Of course not."

It was Rita who demanded quietly, "Why do you ask that?"

"What's the name of the company that insures your jewelry?" I asked.

"I don't see why that concerns you," Rita said. "Diana's already told you we don't want the insurance company brought into this. That's why she hired you."

"I'm not going to inform the insurance company the

pin's been lost," I told them patiently. "But I need some information from them. To find the pin."

It was Diana who told me the name of the insurance company.

My next call was to Ned Baum, a staff claims investigator I knew at that insurance company.

It took Baum a while to dig what I wanted out of the company files. I waited, smoked two Luckies, and fingered the daisy pin. When Baum came back on the line and said he had the list of insured Kosterman gems in his hand, I gave him a detailed description of the pin. It matched a pin described on the insurance list.

"It's insured for full value," Baum told me. "Thirty-one hundred dollars."

Which meant that the pin had once been the real stuff. The company would have had it appraised before issuing insurance on it.

"Anything in your records about a copy ever having been made of this pin?" I asked Baum.

"Nope."

I had him describe the other items of jewelry on the list. There weren't too many pieces, but a few of them, like an emerald necklace and a ruby tiara, were worth hefty sums. All in all, Kosterman had bought one hundred and sixty thousand dollars' worth of jewelry for his present wife, and a little under twenty-five thousand dollars' worth for his daughter.

The daisy pin was the least expensive item on the list.

"What's up?" Baum demanded.

"Nothing for you to worry about."

"You didn't want all this info just to pass the time. If something's doing with these gems, don't let me get caught being the only one not in the know about it."

"I won't," I promised him. "If it looks like somebody's trying a chisel on the insurance, I'll let you know."

After I hung up the phone, I sat a while longer behind my desk, gazing at the daisy pin.

Then I dropped it in my pocket and went out.

* * *

After lunching on a cheeseburger and a milk shake at a drive-in, I began my car prowl of Miami's jewelry establishments. I spent the rest of the afternoon at it, showing the daisy pin each place I went.

Shadows were lengthening into dusk, and I was about ready to call a halt to it for the day, when I entered the basement workshop of Hendrik Ruyter in Hialeah.

Ruyter was a private contractor who did gem cutting and jewel setting for various jewelry firms in the area. He was a small man, with a thick head of white hair and a big apron-covered stomach. When I came down the steps into his little workshop, he was at a bench, fitting a stone into a silver setting.

He looked up at me with a good-natured smile. "Something I can do for you, sir?"

I took out the daisy pin and showed it to him. "Recognize this?"

He took it from me, looked at it, weighed it in his small hand, nodded. "Yes. Of course. This I did a month ago. Maybe a little more." He got out his jeweler's glass and studied the pin through it for a few seconds. Then he dropped the glass back into his apron pocket, gave me back the pin, and nodded again. "Yes."

The weariness of the hours of prowling the city dropped from me. "You're sure?"

"Of course. I always remember my own work. My customer wished the diamonds removed from this setting and these imitation stones substituted. This I did."

"You do much of that kind of work?"

"Some. It is a common job. People buy expensive jewelry. Then they need money. But they don't want their friends to know they have been forced to sell their jewelry. So they take it to a jewelry store, which sends it to me. I substitute imitation gems for the real ones. The people sell the gems to the store, keep the setting with the false stones, and none of their friends are the wiser. A common thing."

"Who'd you do this job for?"

Hendrik Ruyter eyed me for a moment. Still smiling, but cautious, he asked, "You are a policeman?"

I got out my wallet, showed him my credentials.

They were impressive enough for him. "I did this work for Jules Langley."

"Who's he?"

"Jules Langley has a jewelry store in Miami Beach. A new store. He opened it a year ago."

"Where was he before that?"

Ruyter shook his head. "I don't know." He gestured at the daisy pin in my hand. "I did a number of jobs for him like that one. For a couple of months. That was one of the last. Since then, nothing."

One of the answers I'd been seeking was beginning to surface. "Got a record of the work you did for this Jules Langley?"

Ruyter nodded slowly. His eyes were anxious. "This is trouble?"

"Not for you. Let's see those records."

Ruyter shuffled through a doorway at the rear of his basement shop. He came back a minute later with a sheet of paper in his hand and gave it to me.

The descriptions of the jobs Ruyter had done for Langley over a three-month period read like the insurance list Ned Baum had given me over the phone.

Phony gems had been substituted in every item of jewelry owned by Kosterman's wife and daughter.

I stopped at a drugstore in El Portal and bought what I needed to wrap the daisy pin and mail it to my lawyer, Ben Silver, with a note inside for him to hang onto it for me. Then I drove across Biscayne Bay via the Seventy-ninth Street Causeway to Miami Beach, cutting right down Collins Avenue.

Jules Langley's jewelry store was on the fringe of hotel row, on a block of neat tourist-rich shops that shared a single pink-and-baby-blue awning running the length of the pavement. It was the height of the evening trade. Tourists strolled between the tall curb palms and the store fronts, window shopping. All the stores there were open for business, the bright lights from their show windows beckoning.

All except Jules Langley's jewelry store. That was closed. Only a single night lamp burned inside, glinting fitfully on the merchandise in the glass showcases.

I tried the door. It was locked. I knocked loudly. No one appeared inside the empty store. I went into the flower shop next door.

The woman who greeted me as I entered wasn't built right for her tight red slacks and peekaboo red blouse, but she acted like she thought she was.

"Can I help you, sir?" she asked, giving me that old Miami Beach come-on smile. "A corsage? A tropical flower plant for unfortunate friends back North?"

"Got any idea where I can find Jules Langley?"

She lost her come-on smile but remained professionally cordial. "No. I saw him leave about twenty minutes ago. I guess he decided to close up early tonight and go home."

"Where's his home?"

"Search me." She gave me a touch of that old smile. "We're not *that* friendly."

I went out and found a phone booth a block away, looked up Jules Langley's residence address. It was a number out on Okeechobee Road, northwest of Miami. Getting into my Olds, I drove back across the bay.

In the northwest section of the city, near the huge junkyards and metal-product factories, Okeechobee Road joins the narrow Miami Canal that runs straight out into the spooky emptiness of the Everglades. I followed the dark road out beyond the trailer parks and cottage suburbs, out to where the first patches of the wild marshes began. The lights of the city outskirts vanished behind me. Here there were only small individual dwellings spaced far apart in the narrow strip of overgrown land between the road and the canal—ramshackle shacks alternating with neat little bungalows, each with a small boat of some kind moored behind it against the wall of the canal.

Jules Langley's place was a solidly constructed bungalow in a small clearing on the edge of the canal. There was a little metal sign in front, facing the road, with the address on it. I cruised past slowly. The Venetian blinds were all closed, but light showed through from inside. A car was parked between the side of the bungalow and the thick tangle of bushes edging the clearing.

I kept on till the bungalow was out of sight behind me, then pulled the Olds off the road. Snapping off the headlights, I sat there in the dark for a while, listening and thinking. The only sounds came from the crickets and the bullfrogs along the canal.

There was something about the darkness, the locale, and the tension along my nervous system that reminded me unpleasantly of my wanderings through the decaying estate of Dr. Boyd, unaware of Sam trailing me. That had been the second time I'd been ambushed. The first time had been on my own boat. The trouble was that ever since Turpin's phone call I'd been playing blindman's buff with people who all knew the terrain better than I did. In that kind of game, ordinary caution wasn't enough. I needed extra insurance.

I got the insurance out from under the dashboard, stripping off the adhesive tapes that had held it there. It was a tiny .22-caliber repeater automatic. Just four inches long, it looked like a toy. A deadly little toy. The self-ejecting clip held six shots. A short-range emergency weapon.

Working the slide, I pumped the top bullet into the fire chamber, snicked off the safety. I stuffed the little .22 up inside the sleeve of my jacket. It fitted snugly enough to stay there, but a sharp downward jerk of my forearm would shake it into my hand.

I got the .38 out of my belt holster and climbed out of the car. Slowly, warily, I walked back along the weed-choked shoulder of the road.

At the edge of the clearing I stopped, looked around in the moonlight. As far as I could see into the clearing between me and the canal, nothing lurked but the dark, empty night shadows. There was no sound at all from the bungalow, nothing to indicate anyone was home. But the lights still showed through the closed blinds, and the car was still parked by the side wall.

I remained perfectly still for perhaps two minutes, looking and listening. Then I drew a deep, slow breath and stepped into the clearing toward the side of the bungalow.

A voice from the bushes a little behind me to my right froze me. It was a voice I remembered—a whispering voice, taut and nervous.

"I got my sights lined up on your ear, Rome. Empty your hands and lift 'em."

It wasn't entirely unexpected, but my heart lurched anyway. A quiver went the length of my spine. I had to force my fingers to open, letting the .38 thud to the ground. I raised both hands head-high.

The bushes moved. I turned my head slightly to look at him as he emerged with the gun in his hand aimed at me. It was the whisperer who'd used the chloroform sponge on me. The paunchy man with the soured features and the mouth like a locked purse. He halted a safe distance from me. I couldn't make out the expression of his eyes; in the faint moonlight they were just two small dark holes in the shadowed blur of his face. But the gun he had trained on my middle was steady enough to tell me I was going to have to be very, very careful.

Without looking away from me, he called out softly, "Okay, Oscar."

A man rose up from behind the car. The squat, massive thug with the face that looked as if it had been flattened by the foot of an elephant. As he came around the car toward us, the moonlight glinted against the barrel of the gun he carried. And now he had a name: Oscar.

He grinned at the paunchy man and said, "I got to hand it to you, Mr. Langley. You was right all the time."

Jules Langley nodded, not taking the dark holes of his eyes from me. "I was sort of expecting you'd show up, Rome. After Hendrik Ruyter phoned me at the store."

Anger at Ruyter's stupidity stirred in me. "Not very bright of him."

"No," Langley agreed. "Not very. He started yelping

about what kind of dirty business had I handed him and how he wouldn't cover up for me if the cops came around. Not very smart.''

"Shooting me," I said, "wouldn't be smart either. You both forgot to put silencers on those guns this time.''

"There's nobody near enough to hear. But I hope it don't come to that. It will, though, if you make a wrong move. I got something to show you in the house that'll convince you. Let's go.''

Oscar led the way. I followed him, and Langley trailed me. Neither of them was close enough for me to try anything, and Langley's gun eyed the small of my back all the way. They'd done this sort of thing before.

Oscar opened the front door and we went in, Langley shutting the door behind him. They kept out of reach, one on either side of me, their eyes and guns watching me. The living room we entered was large and well furnished, but it didn't look as if Langley had done much living in it. It had the too-neat, uncluttered appearance of a hotel suite used merely as a place to sleep in at night and leave in the morning.

"The bathroom," Langley said. "I want you should see something.''

Oscar plodded across the deep carpet of the living room, past an open bedroom door. He opened the door to the bathroom. Then he moved inside, keeping his gun trained on me. "Have a look.''

"Keep your hands high," Langley warned me, "while you're looking.''

I crossed to the bathroom, with Langley following me, and looked in.

The worn bottoms of a pair of shoes stuck out at me. The shoes were attached to short legs braced stiffly against the sides of the bathtub. In the bathtub, Hendrik Ruyter lay on his back, his arms folded over his chest.

The tub was filled almost to the top. I saw Ruyter's drowned face through the water.

"The guy fell in the canal," snickered Oscar. "Too bad.''

"Now," Jules Langley whispered behind me, "you know I mean business. You know *how much* I mean it. I got no more time to waste. Where's the daisy pin? And where's Nimmo and Catleg?"

Chapter 12

I TURNED AWAY FROM THE BATHROOM. MY STOMACH WAS churning slowly.

"Cute," I mumbled thickly. "Very cute."

"There ain't a mark on him," Langley said. "They'll find him in the canal. Jumped in and drowned himself."

"I won't be that easy," I told him. "You'll have to put a bullet in me first. Maybe more than one. You'll have problems trying to make me look like a suicide."

"There's a stone-crushing plant a couple miles further up the road. We stick you under a pile of stones that's ready for the crusher in the morning. When that crusher gets through with you and that pile of stones, nobody'll ever be able to tell you ate lead first. They won't even be able to be sure you were ever human."

"A little late in the game for you to get that complicated," I said. "How come you just shot Turpin and let him lay?"

"Who's Turpin?"

I frowned at him. Langley wasn't lying. He had no reason to the way things were.

"The guy you shot in my office," I said.

Langley shrugged. "I don't get what you're talking about." He glanced at his massive lieutenant. "Check him, Oscar."

I tensed as Oscar approached me. But Oscar was a professional. "Turn around," he ordered, "and lean against the wall with your hands out."

I did what he told me, turning and tipping my weight forward, catching myself with my palms against the wall. Oscar kept his gun well back in his right hand while his left went through my pockets. He kept to one side, careful not to get between me and Langley's gun. Whatever I tried, a bullet from one or the other of them would get me before I could finish it.

Oscar stepped back from me when he was done. "Not in his pockets, Mr. Langley. But that don't mean nothing. We make him strip, we can be sure."

I pushed myself away from the wall and straightened, turning to face Langley.

He shook his head, studying me. "No. I'm not wasting any more time searching. . . . Rome, last time I didn't know for sure you had it. This time I do. And you're gonna tell me where that pin is. And what happened to Nimmo and Catleg."

"Who're they?"

Oscar slammed the back of his free hand across my face. The force of it smacked me against the wall. My eyes watered from the pain where his big knuckles had struck my nose. I wiped my hand across my upper lip. It came away with a smear of blood.

"Get those hands back up!" Langley snarled.

I raised my hands above my shoulders again. "I don't know any Nimmo. Or Catleg. What makes you think I do?"

"Nimmo was tailing you Saturday," Langley snapped. "You knew me and Oscar. You might've spotted us. So Nimmo had to tail you. With Catleg for protection. That was Saturday. I ain't heard from them since. And this is Monday night."

"So you had a couple guys following me Saturday. This is the first I know about it. Maybe they did a runout on you."

"Uh-uh. Not Nimmo. He's got too big a stake in this. And Catleg'd do what Nimmo told him. Something happened to them. Must've. I figure *you* made it happen."

I expressed part of an idea that was taking hold in me: "What kind of gun does this Nimmo carry?"

"Nimmo? Never carries one. Guns scare him. That's why I had to send Catleg along with him."

"All right. So what kind of gun does Catleg—"

"Dammit!" Langley growled. "I want answers from you, not more questions!"

"It might help me answer," I pointed out softly, "if you tell me what these two characters look like."

Jules Langley eyed me for a moment. "We'll let that one go right now. Maybe you don't know about them. But you do know about that daisy pin. No question about that any more. This is the last time I ask you polite. Where is it?"

I shook my head. "I'd be dumb to tell you. As soon as you have that pin I'm dead."

Oscar slugged me with his fist this time. I saw it coming and moved my head. But not enough. His hard knuckles caught my right eye. I sagged back against the wall. My head spun, then cleared. The flesh over the bruised bone around my eye began to swell.

"Wise guy!" Oscar rasped. "Go on bein' a wise guy. I'll bust your head open for you!"

I straightened and looked at Langley, saying nothing. Both guns were still leveled at my stomach."

"No," Langley said. "That wouldn't work, would it, Rome? You're a tough one. And you know you're gonna die anyway. But there's ways and ways of dying. I give you about fifteen minutes of taking some of the things we can do to you. Fifteen minutes. Then you'll decide to tell me about that pin and go out the easy way. We'll start with taking your eyes out with a penknife. It gets worse after that."

Sweat trickled down my spine. He meant it. It would mean no more to them than drowning Ruyter in the bathtub had.

I sucked in a ragged breath and nodded. "Okay. The pin's in my office."

Langley shook his head, his sour face mean and knowing. "Nuts. The tough ones like you don't quit that easy. You're lying to gain time. You gotta get your dose of pain first. When I see you're soft enough, I'll know you're telling the truth."

He flicked a glance at Oscar. "Get the adhesive tape from the bathroom. We tie him first."

Oscar nodded and started for the open bathroom door. Langley motioned with his head at a heavy ladderback chair beside the sofa. "Sit down there, Rome."

I came away from the wall slowly, moving toward the chair.

Oscar went through the bathroom door and out of sight.

Langley's eyes and gun stayed on me as I moved toward the chair. But, for a few scant seconds, there was only the one pair of eyes. And only the one gun.

I snapped my arms down as I jumped sideways toward the sofa. The roar of Langley's gun filled the room. I felt the bullet tug the back of my jacket as the tiny automatic fell out of my sleeve into my waiting hand. He was bringing his gun around for another shot when I fired. The automatic in my hand made a thin snapping sound.

A short .22 slug doesn't pack much penetration power. But the range was very close. The bullet broke the bridge of Langley's nose and drilled in. Blood welled out, drenching the lower half of his face. He fell over with a gurgling scream, choking on the blood. The gun spilled from his limp fingers.

I spun toward the bathroom as Oscar came out of it. He was still gripped by surprise, trying to understand what was happening, when I shot him. The bullet got him in the midsection. But he was farther away than Langley had been. And with the massive build of his torso, hitting him in the body with a little .22 slug was like trying for an elephant with a deer rifle. It hurt him plenty. But he didn't go down, and he didn't drop his gun.

I snapped the next shot at his face. But by then the pain had shocked him out of his surprised stupor, and he was moving fast. I missed, and then I was all out of surprises. My little weapon jammed on the next trigger pull.

Dropping the useless gun, I got one foot on the cushions of the sofa and vaulted over its back, coming down in a low crouch behind it. Oscar's gun blasted, the slug ripping through the sofa to slash into the floor by my knee.

I scrambled away desperately, reached the bedroom door in a crouch, seized the knob, and opened it. I lunged through, slamming the door shut as Oscar fired again. The bullet tore through the door panel and whined past my ear.

My eyes swept past the closed windows of the bedroom with their drawn blinds and fastened on a tall floor lamp with a brass stand about four feet high. I leaped for it and grabbed it with both hands, ripping its plug out of the wall socket.

Oscar kicked the door open and came charging through, his gun swinging in an arc as he searched for me. I twisted around and swung the long brass lampstand like a baseball bat.

The heavy metal base of the stand caught him square in the middle of the forehead and knocked him back against the wall. There was the sound of splintering bone as the metal base caved in his skull. He slid down the wall and settled on the floor in an unwieldy heap that had no more life to it than a big bag of gravel.

I bent and snatched up his gun, eased nervously through the doorway into the living room, my finger taut across the trigger.

But it was all over.

Jules Langley was dead, sprawled face down in a spreading pool of his own blood that was being rapidly absorbed by the thick nap of the carpet. . . .

I sat on the sofa for what seemed like a long time before I stopped shaking all over. The feeling of nightmarish dizziness took longer to go away. My clothes were drenched with perspiration and plastered to my skin.

When I finally shoved up off the sofa, my legs felt leaden, their muscles feeble, as though I'd just finished a cross-country sprint.

I started toward the bathroom but changed my mind as

I remembered what was in there. Finding the kitchen, I turned on the cold-water spigot and stuck my head under it. When I'd had enough of that, I washed my hands and wrists and gulped down a full tumbler of cold water.

There was a mirror on the wall behind the sink. I looked lousy in it. The flesh around my eye was puffed and was turning purple. The side of my nose was swollen and showed a livid bruise. I took off my jacket and looked at the bullet holes in the back of it.

When I sat down again on the living-room sofa, I was finally beginning to think clearly.

I was in deep. Deeper than deep. I couldn't just walk away from this and leave it for someone else to find. My fingerprints were all over the place. My visit to Ruyter's basement workshop, asking the florist for Langley's address, plus a lot of other things, tied me to the three dead men in that bungalow.

I could level with the cops. Tell them in detail exactly how it had happened from the start. Maybe they would get to believe me after a while. But that meant I'd have to admit holding back information after Turpin's murder. The cops could manage to make some kind of charge against me stick if they tried. They'd be in a mood to try.

I'd gotten in this deep because I'd tried to protect Rudolph Kosterman and his family. Not out of altruism. I didn't kid myself about that. Kosterman was the big client who could lead to more big clients. I'd smelled all those fat fees waiting for me, and I'd stepped into a hole.

Well, the situation had changed. I was willing to let go of Kosterman now if it was the only way to save my own skin. But now I couldn't let go. Now I needed Kosterman's help as much as he needed mine. Maybe more.

I used the phone to call Kosterman's home. It didn't matter now whether the cops later traced the call or not. The butler answered and got Kosterman for me.

"I was hoping you'd call, Rome," Kosterman said when he came on. "I tried to reach you at your office today. Several times."

"I've been kept busy," I said, "with your problems."

"That's what I called you about. You can forget all about my problems. I don't have them any more. Except that the people I love most for some reason seem to be afraid to tell me what's bothering them. But that's over with, too. I believe the check I sent you should cover any work you've done for me."

Something cold and hard formed in the pit of my stomach. "Come again?" I muttered.

"What's the matter? Can't you hear me?"

"I hear you, Mr. Kosterman. I just don't understand you."

"I hired you," he said impatiently, "to find out what was troubling Diana. Well, I've found out."

"How?"

"Darrell has told me. He's been restless and unhappy, and he admits he's taken it out on Diana."

"The business about not feeling like his own man because he works for his father-in-law?"

"Yes," Kosterman said. "If you knew, why didn't you tell me? Oh, well . . . it's better this way Diana and Darrell telling me themselves. They dropped by my office together this evening just before my wife came by to pick me up. They told me, and we're all feeling better as a result. I think Darrell is making a mistake, but I can certainly understand his feeling the way he does. He's learned enough about selling development houses to make a try on his own. And of course I'll help when he'll let me."

"So everybody's happy now? Including your daughter?"

"Sure. Confession is good for the soul, they say. And—"

"Did she tell you about the daisy pin?"

"Yes. She told me she lost it. It was ridiculous of her not to tell me before. There's nothing so upsetting about that. I'll call the insurance company in the morning and report it. They'll either find it or give me the money it's worth."

"Are you sure you want to do that?"

Kosterman was silent for a moment. He was smart

enough to know I wasn't asking a question like that just to prolong the conversation.

"What do you mean?" he asked.

"I found the pin your daughter lost," I told him. "Only it's a phony."

There was a slight pause at the other end. Then he said, "What do you mean, a phony? My daughter's jewelry is real enough. You must be wrong."

"The diamonds were removed from the pin and phony stones substituted. The same thing's been done to every piece of jewelry your wife and daughter have."

"Are you sure?"

"I'm sure."

"But, who . . ."

"That's the interesting question," I said.

There was a longer pause while he thought it over. "Can you come right out here, Rome?"

"Uh-huh. Your wife there?"

"Yes."

"How about your daughter and son-in-law?"

"They're getting ready to leave for—"

"Keep them there," I told him, and hung up.

Outside the bungalow I found my .38 where I'd dropped it and stuck it back in the belt holster. Then I got into the Olds and drove away.

The farther north I drove, the less real the contents of that bungalow seemed to me. But those dead men *were* real—and there was an invisible wire attaching each one of them to me.

It was only a matter of time before the cops started to follow those strands to me.

We were all in the den in Kosterman's mansion. Diana and Darrell Pines sat together on one of the couches. Rita Kosterman perched on the edge of a wide chair next to them. Rudolph Kosterman paced. I leaned against the fireplace wall and tried to watch all of them at once.

My short, pointed tale about murders and dead men had shocked them. But no one among them seemed to be taking it noticeably harder than the others. As a matter of fact, they all took much harder my news about the switched gems. And there again, no one of them appeared less surprised about it than the others.

"You *could* be wrong," Kosterman said.

"Take the jewelry to a jeweler in the morning," I said. "But make sure he's a discreet one. I'm not wrong."

"But how could it happen?"

"One way. Somebody takes one piece of jewelry at a time to a crooked jeweler. The genuine stones are removed and fake gems put in their place. The piece of jewelry is returned, and it's time for our somebody to lift another piece. Till it's been done to all the jewelry in this house."

"You keep saying *somebody*," Kosterman snapped. "Who?"

I shrugged a shoulder. "Any one of you here." I looked steadily at Kosterman. "You, for instance. How's business?"

For a moment I thought his wife Rita was going to come off her chair clawing. "Are you crazy?" she flared furiously. "Accusing a man like Rudy! He'd never stoop to such—"

Kosterman silenced her with a sharp gesture of his hand. "Maybe I would. If I needed the dough—bad and fast. I'd find me a crooked jeweler and split what the gems were worth with him. I *might* do something like that if I had to. I've seen dirtier angles than that worked."

He turned slightly to look fully at me. "But right now business is fine."

I looked at the others, at the anger in their faces as they waited for what they knew I'd say next. I said it slowly: "Then it could be your wife. Or your daughter. Or your son-in-law."

Darrell Pines stood up and took a step toward me. "I almost tangled with you a few nights ago, Rome. This time I will."

"Darrell!" Kosterman roared.

His son-in-law stopped dead in his tracks.

"It seems to me," Kosterman said to him, "that for a

young man so anxious to control his own business, you don't have much control over *yourself*. We're not playing games here. Something is happening in this family, and we're trying to find out what it is.''

Darrell Pines actually blushed. He sat down beside his young wife again. Diana took one of his hands in both of hers and squeezed it reassuringly. She looked at me.

"Why does it have to be one of us?" she demanded. "Couldn't it be one of the servants?"

"Not likely. Before I brought you home Friday night, your father got all the servants out of the way. None of them could have known you lost your pin till the next day. Yet when I got back to my boat that night, Jules Langley and his muscle boy were waiting for me, looking for that pin. The only ones who could have known the pin was missing that soon and phoned Langley about it were you four. And Anne Archer. I rule her out. She doesn't live here. She wouldn't have been able to get the jewelry to Langley and back where it belonged here, one item at a time. That means it has to be one of you four.''

Rudolph Kosterman looked slowly from his wife to his daughter to his son-in-law. He drew a deep breath and looked at me.

"All right, Rome. You're still working for me. At double the original fee. Find out how it happened, and why. When you know, you'll tell me. No one else. I'm not reporting it to the insurance company nor filing any claims. So it remains a purely family matter. It has to remain that.''

"There've been a couple of murders," I pointed out softly. "Ralph Turpin and Hendrik Ruyter. If anyone here is in any way responsible for either of those deaths, I won't be able to keep it a private family secret.''

"I understand that," Kosterman said. "I also understand that you will do what you can to spare me and my family. There'll be a sizable bonus for you if you succeed.''

"I'll have to tell the cops about the jewelry being stolen and the gems switched," I told him. "But I don't have to let them have what I just told you—that one of your family is involved. They may guess it. But as long as I don't give them the facts I have that prove it, they can't act on it or give it out to the newspapers. They'll have to treat it like a simple outside job of burglary by Langley. The fact that it's an inside job stays with the five of us.''

Kosterman nodded slowly, waiting for me to say more.

We eyed each other steadily. We both understood the meanings beneath the polite words. He was offering me a bribe to commit any crime necessary to get his family off the hook. And I was suggesting that I'd get it done. I was doing something else, too: I was setting him up for a request of my own—though I wasn't ready to spring that for a few moments.

My nerves were screaming at me. There were three dead men waiting for me, and if anyone else discovered them before I reported it I was finished.

But I had to play it cool with Kosterman. I couldn't let him suspect the state of my nerves. The rich, no matter how decent any of them may be in other ways, all share a peculiarity. Too many people seek favors from them, so they acquire an allergy to all favor-seekers. I had to keep Kosterman feeling it was all the other way around.

I looked at Rita, Diana, and Pines. ''There's one way we might be able to keep it in the family. Whichever one of you slipped the jewels to Langley could say so right now. And I'll do what I can for you.''

I waited. They stared back at me. All three looked guilty as hell, in the way anyone accused will.

When none of them answered, I said, ''All right, do any of you know a man called Nimmo? Or one named Catleg?''

None of them had anything to say to that either.

I looked at Kosterman. I wanted to get the last of it over with, but I knew I had to play it just right. When you're trying to stick the game out with a half bluff, hoping for luck to improve your hand, you can't let your anxiety show.

''I'll do what I can,'' I said and started out of the room.

Then I stopped and turned back to him as though a stray thought had hit me.

"By the way, Mr. Kosterman, in a couple hours I'm going to have cops crawling in and out of my pockets. They'll want to toss me in a cell. They'll want a scapegoat until they can straighten things out and find a guilty party— and I'm a natural for the job. I held things from them to shield you. Now they'll know it. I won't be much use to you in a cell. And with enough pressure, I might be forced to talk."

"I see," Kosterman said quietly. "Naturally, I wouldn't want that to happen."

Once more, the words were just a cover for what we were really saying to each other. And we still understood each other very well. I was practically blackmailing him, to get myself off the hook. If he'd see to it I stayed free, I'd keep from the cops the facts that proved one of his family was involved in the gem switch. And I could see by his expression that I'd succeeded. It was a trade.

I said, "All right, then. If you've got any strings you can pull in Dade County and Miami . . ."

I knew, of course, that he did have the strings to pull. No man could get rich in Florida in his line of business without acquiring some political leverage.

Kosterman nodded. "I'll begin making some phone calls right away. How much of this mess do I have to reveal?"

"Just that I'm working for you. And you want me free to continue doing so."

Back in my Olds, the first thing I did was get the flask out of the glove compartment and take a couple stiff slugs from it. I waited till the brandy took hold. Then I drove back to that death-filled bungalow on the Miami Canal.

Everything was as I'd left it. Ruyter in the bathtub, Langley on the living room carpet, and Oscar in the bedroom.

I used the bungalow phone to call Santini at Miami homicide. The bungalow was outside Miami limits, in county territory, which made it a matter for the sheriff's metro police. But the deaths there were connected with Turpin's killing. Besides, Santini was the nearest thing to a friend that I was likely to find among the cops that night.

After hanging up the phone I waited ten minutes to give Santini a head start. Then I called the metro police.

Then I waited.

Chapter 13

FOR THE REST OF THE NIGHT THERE WERE MORE VARIETIES of cops climbing all over me than you'd find at a policemen's convention.

You won't find a law setup anywhere that's more complicated than what we've got in Greater Miami and Dade County. Including Miami and scattered around it are twenty-six independent incorporated communities, some with less than five hundred citizens but each with its own police force. Twisting through and around these communities is unincorporated county territory, which is policed by the sheriff's metropolitan cops.

They converged on me from all parts of that crazy setup: the metro cops because the bungalow was in county territory; Miami cops because I worked there and Turpin had died there; cops from Hialeah, where Hendrik Ruyter had worked and lived; cops from Miami Beach, where Jules Langley had his jewelry store. Plus Petrov and another assistant from the district attorney's office, a medical examiner, the emergency squad, the fingerprint boys, an official photographer from the sheriff's office, a couple of police secretaries, and a representative from the state police.

Hour after hour, I was questioned, pushed, pulled, threatened, cajoled. My better instincts were appealed to; my baser fears were tapped. I told my story so many times, to so many badges that it began to sound like the mechanical recitation of a memorized prayer—which, in a way, it was.

I got a little help from an unexpected quarter: the Miami Beach police. They'd been keeping an eye on Jules Langley lately. According to them, the things of which I was accusing the late Langley were quite possible.

It was his connections with the hustlers and more elegant B-girls of Miami Beach that had first attracted the attention of the Beach cops. Langley was working an old racket, one so close to being legal that it was impossible to nail him for it. It was not unusual for a wealthy tourist to get a real yen for one of the luscious creatures working the bars along the Beach and decide to win her with an item of expensive jewelry. When this happened, the girl made sure the sucker bought the jewelry from Jules Langley. Later, of course, she returned the jewelry to Langley for a commission.

The wallet-milking lovelies of the Miami Beach nights were too much of a prime tourist attraction for the cops to care much about this. What did interest them was a growing suspicion that Langley was involved with some of the gem smuggling for which Miami is a center. The suspicion had been strong enough to set them digging into his background.

Langley had come to Miami Beach from New York a year and a half before, bringing Oscar with him. According to the New York cops, Oscar had done time for various activities ranging from breaking-and-entering to manslaughter. Langley had had a jewelry store near Times Square. He'd sold out and moved South to more tolerant terrain when the New York cops began pressuring him for working his jewelry-gift-commission racket with a couple of the Manhattan call-girl outfits.

This information about the unsavory pasts of Langley and Oscar helped make my story a bit more believable. But it didn't noticeably lift any of the weight of the law off me.

At six in the morning, groggy and bone-weary, I was taken to one of the sheriff's offices in the Dade County

Courthouse in Miami. The number of cops I carried with me had dwindled by then, but they still made a roomful: Petrov, a metro captain, Art Santini, the sheriff's special homicide investigator, and a police secretary.

None of them acquired any liking for me in the next few hours. The irritating factor, from their viewpoint, was that nothing I said gave them a tangible case to work on. Yet everything I told them checked out as far as they could check it. They hadn't enough evidence to pin anything on me and make it stick, and we all knew it. But there was enough there for them to rig something against me, and we all knew that too.

They tried the hard approach and the soft, and both at the same time. Unofficially, I was charged with everything from murder to withholding information in a felony. My answers to their questions remained the same. I stuck stubbornly to my story and sat tight, waiting for the political juice that Kosterman was supposed to be generating to reach me.

Essentially, what I told them was the truth—or as much of it as I'd been able to piece together:

Jules Langley had managed to get hold of the Kosterman jewels, substitute imitations for the real gems, and return them without their ever being missed. It was a neat, painless steal. Because the gems had never been reported stolen, Langley could peddle them for their full value, instead of the cut-rate prices that hot stones bring. He was even able to give the job of switching the real gems for phonies to a legitimate contractor like Ruyter instead of to an underworld gem setter who'd have charged him ten times as much.

It was profit without peril for Langley until Diana Pines lost the daisy pin. Somehow, Langley learned about her losing it and got worried. Whoever had the pin would find out it was a fake, and that might lead to uncovering what Langley had done. He'd tried to get the pin back fast— first through me on Friday night, then by having two men named Nimmo and Catleg tail me on Saturday.

I didn't know who they were, and the names meant

nothing to the cops. But my hunch on one of them leaned to the man I'd run into as I was leaving Turpin's hotel room that Saturday: the darkly handsome, fortyish man, with the graying black hair and the scar under his left eye. If he was Nimmo or Catleg, he'd overheard me accusing Turpin of having the daisy pin.

Turpin *was* the one who'd lifted the pin from Diana Pines, of course. He'd taken it to Sands for appraisal that Saturday morning. After I left, Turpin went back to Sands and learned the pin was worthless. It must have struck Turpin as funny that I'd offered him a hundred dollars to return a worthless pin. He mailed it to me and went back to his hotel room.

Meanwhile somebody, probably Catleg and Nimmo, had searched Turpin's room for that pin, working too fast to be neat about it. Turpin had returned, found the mess, and assumed I'd done the search job to get out of paying him his hundred bucks. Sore as a boil, he'd headed for my office and got there five or ten minutes after I'd left with Diana Pines.

Catleg—maybe together with Nimmo—had tailed Turpin to my office, figuring Turpin had gone there to return the daisy pin to me personally. If my guess was right, Catleg had to be tailing Turpin, whether with Nimmo or without him. Because according to Langley, Nimmo carried no gun.

Catleg—again *maybe* with Nimmo—walked in after Turpin, waving a gun at him. Now, Turpin wasn't what you'd call brave. He was too hotheaded to ever get scared enough to have to exercise bravery. He had a fast temper and a fast gun hand. He must have gone for his own gun, got it out, and fired it before he was shot.

Langley never heard from Catleg or Nimmo again. But wherever they went, one of them went with Turpin's .45 slug deep in him.

On Monday morning, I got the pin Turpin had mailed me and found it was a phony. Checking all the jewelry outfits led me to Hendrik Ruyter—and the information about the jobs he'd done for Jules Langley.

After I'd left Ruyter, he made his fatal mistake. He was furious at the thought that Langley might have used him for something illegal, and he'd called Langley and told him so. Langley closed up his shop before I got there, took Oscar with him, and sped to Hialeah. They picked up Ruyter, took him to Langley's bungalow, and drowned him in the tub. Then they waited for me to show up.

And that was my story.

Of course, I left out a few things.

I didn't mention the fact that the Kosterman jewels had been lifted, worked on, and returned one at a time, over a period of a couple of months—because that would have told the cops someone in the Kosterman family was in on it.

I neglected to tell them I had a lead to the man called Nimmo.

And I didn't say anything about my hunch that Langley had been planning a follow-up gimmick that would have doubled his already sizable take from the Kosterman jewels. My hunch would explain his getting so upset about the missing daisy pin. And it was such a logical follow-up that I couldn't see how he could let the opportunity pass.

My guess was that he was planning to have his confederate in the Kosterman home toss all the jewels in the ocean and make it look like an outside robbery. The jewels wouldn't be found and the insurance company would have to make good to Kosterman. He'd use the dough to replace the missing jewelry. Then Langley could pull the original gimmick again: put phonies into the jewelry and pocket the real gems.

This hunch made me feel a bit better about Ruyter's death. If I was right, he'd been scheduled to die even if I hadn't come along. For once the jewelry was reported stolen, the cops and insurance agents would have started asking around for them. Langley must have planned to do away with Ruyter so he couldn't tell the cops anything, when the time came. I'd just speeded up the doing of it.

The cops in that office with me were all smart enough

to sense the soft spots in my story, and they slapped me with them.

I stuck to my version.

At nine thirty Tuesday morning, when the mail arrived at the office of Ben Silver, my lawyer, a metro sergeant was there to pick up the package I'd sent. The daisy pin was appraised and bore out that part of my story at least.

By ten A.M. the cops with me were almost as exhausted as I was. They decided it was time to give me the waiting-and-worrying treatment. I was transferred to a lone cell on the seventeenth floor.

The jail, which takes up the sixteenth to nineteenth floors in the Dade County Courthouse, is not noted for comfortable accommodations. The beds consist of iron slabs—but I had weariness to cushion me. Two minutes after stretching out on that cold, hard metal, I was sound asleep.

I had to be awakened by the Negro trusty who brought my lunch. I wolfed down every ounce of the slop and went back to oblivion.

By suppertime I was slept out and beginning to feel the bruises from my iron mattress. I ate with less appetite than before. Then I started putting in nervous time. I chain-smoked the rest of my package of Luckies and began gnawing on a thumbnail.

It was almost eight o'clock Tuesday evening when I was finally taken out of the cell and back down to that office in the sheriff's department.

This time the only one waiting for me was Art Santini. He sat behind the desk, eying me as I came in. On top of the desk was my .38 in the clip-on holster, my wallet, keys, and the other items they'd lifted from me.

I grinned at Santini. "I guess you had a talk with Kosterman."

"In a way," he snapped. "We talked to him—through the Mayport chief of police. The chief there's in Kosterman's pocket."

"I guess he's not the only one," I said, gesturing at my things on the desk. "I take it I'm released."

"Yeah," Santini said bitterly. "The word came down. Lay off Kosterman, and let you go. Unless we've got something solid on you. We don't. Not solid enough . . . not yet."

I sighed and started collecting my things. "It's nice to have rich, influential friends."

"Is it? Your father didn't think so at the end."

I was picking up my .38 when he said that. For a few seconds I was still as stone, holding the gun in my hands and looking at Santini.

"We've been friends," I said finally. "And you're upset. I'll forget you said it. This time."

"I wouldn't if I were you," Santini said, meeting my stare angrily. "I'd remember it. It's quite an object lesson. You cover up the dirt for a man like Kosterman, and in the end he comes out clean and *you* wind up with all the dirt."

I did the job of fastening the .38 holster to my belt slowly, mechanically, studying Santini. "You *are* worked up."

"What'd you expect? We all are. That's why they gave me this little task. They figured I was the only one who might not take a sock at you. I'm not sure they were right."

"What're you all so sore about?"

His mouth opened in surprise. "Are you kidding, Tony? You think we don't know you aren't being straight with us? You think we don't realize somebody in Kosterman's house had to be working with Jules Langley? But you hold out on us, make it harder for us to do a job that's tough enough anyway. You get Kosterman to pull strings for you, so some lousy politicians start telling us what we can do and can't do. How do you expect us to feel about you?"

"All right, you sanctimonious bastard," I told him softly, "let's play this for keeps. I'll make a bargain with you. I'll give you anything I've held back. It isn't much, but you can have it."

His eyes narrowed suspiciously. "And what's my end of the bargain?"

"Just ignore the word that came down from the political boys. You've got a duty to do. Do it."

"Like what?" He knew what I meant. He wasn't enjoying it.

"You think somebody in Kosterman's house was tied in with Jules Langley. I agree with you, but I don't know which one any more than you do. But you can find out easier than I can. Just pull 'em all in. Kosterman. His wife. His daughter and son-in-law. Sweat each one of them separately. I guarantee you the guilty one'll let it slip inside two hours. Between you and all the other law around here that's so sore at me, you can pull it off. Nothing can stop you."

Santini's fists were clenched on the edge of the desk. He gazed down at them, his face coloring. "My job wouldn't be worth a plugged nickel afterwards," he muttered weakly.

"Sure," I agreed. "You're thinking about your future. And I was thinking about mine. But I'm willing to forget that if you are. I'll stop tidying up Kosterman's troubles. You stop knuckling under just because he's passed down the word. A bargain?"

"Okay, okay," he growled. "You made your point. Now get out of here, will you?"

I got out of there.

Chapter 14

A CALYPSO BAND BESIDE THE CANDY-STRIPED BAR ON THE hotel terrace filled the night air with its singing and playing. Guests in tuxedos and evening gowns danced to the music under coconut palms strung with multicolored lights. I skirted the terrace and made my way past the glass-walled hotel night club, along a fragrant, hibiscus-bordered tile walk to the hotel's cabana club, which faced the dark beach.

More decorated palms lined the deserted sunbathers' lanai. The pool, embraced by its semicircle of Moorish-design cabanas, had concealed colored lights below the surface, which tinted the clear water with blue and red, green and yellow. Anne Archer was poised on the low board at the other end of the pool. I watched her go up on her toes and dive off, cutting cleanly into the water with hardly a splash. She glided through the length of the pool, breaststroking smoothly.

She surfaced at my end gasping for air. Grasping the iron rungs of the pool ladder, she climbed out shedding drops of water like a small rain. Freckles dotted her shoulders. She wore a tight golden bathing cap and a one-piece swimsuit of jersey that clung to the soft fullness of her curves, emphasizing them spectacularly. Her legs were even longer than I'd remembered, but just as exquisite.

"My God," she said when she saw me standing there. "You look horrible."

"Sorry. I wanted to catch you before you went out for the night. I didn't take time to shave and change."

"I don't mean that. You look like you've been in a brawl."

I touched the tender bruise alongside my nose, the puffed area around my eye. "It was pretty one-sided as you can see. I've got some questions to ask you."

"I should be getting used to that." Her red hair tumbled down in damp waves as she stripped off her cap.

"Got a little time before your date?"

"I don't have a date tonight," she said, picking up a white terrycloth robe from one of the candy-striped beach mats and slipping into it. "Matter of fact, I didn't really have one the last time you came around."

"Why'd you say you did?"

She shrugged, belting her robe. "Female training. Make the man eager through jealousy. It didn't work out very well."

"I guess I'm just not competitive enough."

"Let's go up to my rooms," she said. "I'm shivering. They warm the water, and the air is cool."

We took the pool elevator up to her floor. In her living room she murmured, "Make yourself comfortable," and vanished into the bedroom.

I lit a Lucky and waited. When she came back she was in white slacks and a white Russian blouse, her hair piled atop her head and held there by an ornamental silver comb. She hadn't put on make-up and she looked prettier that way. The red hair, green eyes, and golden freckles were coloring enough for her.

"You look worse in the light," Anne commented factually, surveying me. "Where'd you get so rumpled and dirty?"

"In jail."

Her eyes widened. "You've been in jail? Honestly?"

"Uh-huh. All day. I just got out."

"But . . . does that sort of thing happen to you often in your line of work?"

"It happens." I gave her one of my cigarettes and lit it for her.

She took a deep drag at it, blew out a cloud of smoke, and studied me interestedly. "I've never met anyone just out of jail before. I'll bet you could use a drink."

I shook my head. "I could use some information about a guy called Nimmo."

It startled her. "Nimmo?"

"The last time I was up here you got a phone call. About somebody with that name."

"Sure," she said slowly. "I remember. But what makes that your business?" She wasn't annoyed, just curious.

"Saturday a Miami hotel detective who used to be my partner was murdered. I think Nimmo is involved. It's not a common name."

It took her a moment to adjust. "Nimmo Fern?"

"I don't know." I described the tall, darkly handsome man I'd run into outside Turpin's hotel room. "Early forties. A short, broad scar under this eye." It could have been Catleg—but luck was with me.

Anne nodded excitedly. "That's him all right. Nimmo Fern. That's some coincidence. My knowing him, and you thinking he's involved in a murder."

"In this case," I told her, "I don't think there's really much coincidence involved."

"What do you mean?"

"Where does this Nimmo Fern live?"

"Search me."

"Where can I find him?"

"I don't know. I haven't seen Nimmo in over a month."

I snubbed my cigarette out in an ashtray and got a grip on my impatience. "All right. Just tell me what you know about him."

"Like what?"

"Who is he? What is he? For a start."

"I'm not sure," Anne said hesitantly. "I got the impression he's some kind of lone-wolf gambler. He talked a lot about the gambling in Las Vegas and Havana."

"How'd you meet him?"

"It was about a week after I came down here to wait out my divorce. I was awfully restless—I needed something to keep me from feeling sorry for myself. Something exciting, different. One of the bellhops recommended Floring's Place. Know it?"

I nodded. "Plush night club up near The Strip."

"There's a secret gambling room in the back of the club. Did you know that?"

"I've heard rumors. Floring must have some heavy connections. The Beach cops've been cracking down on gambling lately."

"Floring keeps it pretty exclusive. You need an introduction to get in the back room. The bellhop was nice enough to call up Floring and fix it so I could get in."

"That was nice of him all right. He gets a fat rake-off for steering loot-heavy people like you to a joint like that."

Anne grinned crookedly. "I suppose so. Well, I went on a sort of gambling binge there for a couple of weeks till I calmed down. And that's where I met Nimmo Fern. He showed me how to recoup some of my losses by making side bets at the craps table. After that we began seeing each other from time to time."

"If you dated him, you must have some idea where to get in touch with him."

She shook her head. "I don't. He'd just phone me from someplace and ask for a date. I think he was impressed with me, liked being seen out with me." She gave me that defensive look again. "I don't think I was the kind of woman he was used to."

"Sure. Where'd you usually meet him?"

"Here. Or at the bar in Floring's Place."

"He never told you anything about where he was from, where he worked?"

"No. And I never asked. He was that kind of man. He talked about all the places he'd been and hinted he was in the rackets. He knew that made him more interesting. But outside of that, he never said much about himself."

I asked if she knew a man named Catleg. She didn't. I

sighed and paced to the windows and looked out at the white, frothy combers surging on the beach.

"You say you haven't seen Nimmo Fern in over a month. How come?"

Anne shrugged and looked a little embarrassed. "His charm wore thin after a while. What was fascinating about him began to seem a little sinister. And I began to realize he actually had a lot of contempt for women. All women. Explanation enough?"

I nodded. "What was that phone call about?"

"That was Seth, the piano player at Floring's. He wanted to know if I'd seen Nimmo lately. He said he owed Nimmo some money and wanted to pay it back, but Nimmo hadn't been around the past few days."

I thought about that for a few seconds. "Tell me. Did Nimmo ever meet any of the Kosterman family as far as you know?"

"Once. I was invited to a beach party Diana threw on The Island. I took Nimmo along."

I felt something quicken in me. "How long ago was this?"

Anne thought back. "About four months ago . . . yes. It was a couple of weeks after I met Nimmo."

"Any of them act like they knew him? Or did he say anything about knowing any of them from before?"

"No. Why? They wouldn't be likely to know somebody like Nimmo."

"You wouldn't think so," I mused. "How'd they take him?"

"Oh . . . Diana and Darrell thought he was pretty fascinating. Rita seemed to take an instant dislike to him though."

"How do you know?" I asked quickly. "Did she say anything to him?"

"Not to him. To me. She said she was disappointed in my choice of men." A light blush suffused Anne's cheeks. She looked away from me, chewing her lower lip. "After that Rita made herself scarce for the rest of the party."

"How'd Kosterman like Nimmo?"

"Rudy wasn't there that day." Anne took another of my cigarettes, lit it off the tip of her old one. "I told Nimmo what Rita said about him, after we left. Trying to get a rise out of him. He only laughed."

She crushed out her second cigarette after only a couple of puffs and looked at me again. "Do I get told the rest of what all this is about? Or do you have to go on being mysterious?"

I thought for a moment and made up my mind. "Look, you said you didn't like short notice, but you don't have a date tonight. How about going out with me to Floring's Place?"

"I wish I was dumb enough to think that's a social invitation," Anne said. "You want to ask Floring about Nimmo, right?"

I nodded. "And that piano player, Seth."

She heaved a mock sigh. "Okay, Tony, I'll pretend it was sweet of you to ask me."

I went to the *Straight Pass* for a shower, shave and change of clothes. Then drove back to pick Anne up. By the time we reached Floring's, the night's business was in full bloom.

The main front room of Floring's Place was big, crowded, noisy. Smoke from dozens of cigarettes fogged its purplish lighting. Tables and chairs hugged the walls on which had been painted murals depicting an adolescent boy's idea of life in a harem. There was a circular bar in the center of the room, with a small raised stage inside it. A four-piece combo was pounding out a rhythm with a primitive beat, while an awkward but gorgeously formed young stripper shed her complicated clothing arrangement on the stage and tried to move her hips to the music at the same time. Equally leggy strippers who had finished their numbers or were waiting to go on hustled drinks from lone males at the bar. The customers, exhibiting every possible degree of tan and sunburn, seemed to be having a grand time. They felt they had to, at a dollar fifty for a small glass of beer.

We sat at one of the tables near the wall. I ordered brandy on the rocks for both of us, and Anne asked the waiter to tell Floring she'd like to see him.

The drinks arrived first. While we were sipping and waiting, the stripper finished peeling and the band took a short break. Anne called to Seth, the piano player. He came to our table, said "Hi, Mrs. Archer," gave me a fast smile, and slumped in a chair. He was a weedy young man wearing dark sunglasses, thin golden hair, and the careworn expression of an accountant at income-tax time.

"Man, I'm done," he rasped. "Can I have a gin?"

"They got the musicians hustling drinks too, now?" I asked him.

He gave me a pained look. "No, man, I'm talking about real gin. I need it. I'm tapering the monkey off my back. Okay?"

I nodded. He grabbed a passing waiter and ordered a double gin, no ice.

"I'm looking for Nimmo Fern," I told him. "Mrs. Archer says you are, too."

"I *was*. No more."

"You found him?"

"Uh-uh. He ain't been around. For which praise Allah. I owe him some loot. I had it when I called Mrs. Archer. Hour later I got cleaned in a craps game. Now I couldn't pay him dime one."

His drink arrived. He gulped it like water.

"Think Nimmo'll be sore about your not being able to pay?" I asked him.

"I ain't looking forward, I'll tell you true. He's got that mean look, you know?"

"I owe him too," I said. "Got any idea where I can find him?"

"Who can ever find Nimmo? He finds you, like. That's why they call him Nimmo. Most of the time, he ain't."

I asked if he knew anybody named Catleg. He said he didn't.

A big, tuxedoed man whose pale round face and bald skull had never been subjected to a drop of the famed

Miami sun drifted to our table and smiled down at us benignly.

"Good to see you again, Mrs. Archer. Been a while."

"Hello, Mr. Floring," Anne said. "Can you join us for a minute?"

Floring's smile widened. "My pleasure." He flicked a look at Seth that would have chopped down a tree. Seth got up hastily, mumbled, "Time for the next number," and vanished. Floring sat in the vacated chair and gave me a pleasant, curious smile.

"This," Anne said, gesturing at me, "is . . . a very good friend of mine, Mr. Floring."

"Any friend of Mrs. Archer's," he said, and shook my hand with the crusher grip that's somehow supposed to indicate friendly intent. "You like to gamble?"

"Too much," I told him truthfully. "I owe Nimmo Fern some money, but I can't find him to pay off. Anne thought you might know where to reach him."

Floring shook his head regretfully. "Sorry. He hasn't been around here in over a week."

"Have you known Nimmo long?"

"A while. Why?"

"Well . . ." I pretended embarrassment. "It was quite a lot of money he won from me. I just wondered if you considered him honest."

"I'd say he's a straight enough gambler," Floring told me, considering it. "At least, I've never heard about anybody accusing him of cheating yet. And I've known him almost since he first came here about a year ago."

"Oh? He's not native Miami?"

"Him? Naw."

"Where's he from? I couldn't place his accent."

Floring shrugged. "Who knows where gamblers come from? Sometimes I think they were all born and grew up on a plane between Las Vegas and Havana."

"Any idea where I can find him?" I asked.

He shook his head. "Nimmo's a pretty shut-mouthed guy. Hard to know anything about."

"Can you think of anybody who might know?"

"Well . . . Georgia might."

"Who?"

"Georgia McKay. One of my strippers. She always acts pretty buddy-buddy with him."

I glanced toward the bar. "Which one is she?"

"Georgia ain't here now. She took off early with a big wallet from Baltimore. He said."

"That was pretty generous of you," I said, "letting her off for the night."

Floring laughed. "Generous, hell! He bought two magnums of champagne to pry her loose from here. At a hundred ten a bottle I can miss her for one night. Not that it'll do that poor sucker any good."

"What do you mean?"

He grinned. "She's a . . ." He glanced at Anne, then back to me. "She don't like men. She's probably ditched him by now, and he's eating his heart out. Can't say I blame him. She's a real stacked chip."

"Where do I find her?"

"She lives in a trailer camp out on Northwest Thirty-sixth." He gave me the address. I thanked him and paid the check.

"She probably ain't home yet," Floring said as we rose. He glanced winningly at Anne. "How about you and your friend visiting the back room for a while? I don't mind losing money to nice people like you."

Anne grinned at him. "You've got a nerve saying that after all the money I've dropped here."

"Only one way to get even, you know," Floring intoned. "Luck can't always go one direction. It's got to turn. Science says so."

"My bank account says otherwise," Anne told him.

I tried the name Catleg on him, but it didn't ring a bell. So I told him we'd be around for a try at his back room another time. That got us loose from him.

Out in my car, I turned to Anne. "I'd better take it alone from here on."

"Well, I guess it's safe enough to let you. Floring did say she doesn't like men."

I dropped her off at her hotel.

"Take care," Anne said quietly as she got out of the car. "Don't go getting yourself beaten up again. Don't get thrown in any more jails."

I solemnly promised to do my best to avoid both pitfalls.

After she vanished into the hotel lobby, I pulled away from the curb and drove to meet the luscious, unattainable Miss Georgia McKay.

Chapter 15

EXCEPT FOR THE WHEELS UNDER THE TRAILERS, THERE was nothing about the community which suggested impermanence. The trailers were arranged in neat rows like houses on a block, each with its own small landscaped plot, its own little garden, and a tiny patio shaded by a colored aluminum ramada or a gaily striped awning. Some trailers were even flanked by children's swings and slides.

Georgia McKay's trailer was one of the boxcar-sized Great Lakes jobs, propped up at both ends with cement blocks, near the kidney-shaped swimming pool. Most of the residents had already turned in for the night, but lamplight showed through the Venetian blinds of Georgia McKay's trailer. I knocked at the front door and waited.

It was a minute before the door was opened. The woman who opened it wore a nondescript man's bathrobe and shapeless slippers. Her mousy brown hair, about the length of a man's when he's three weeks overdue at the barber's, was tousled. She was stocky, her face broad and stolid. Her sleepy eyes blinked at me. She rasped, "What is it?"

I asked, "Georgia McKay?"—but I knew she couldn't be.

"No. I'm Irma. Georgia's roommate. What do you want?"

"I'm looking for someone Georgia knows. Floring thought she might be able to help me find him."

"Floring sent you?" Irma eyed me suspiciously. "But she's still at Floring's Place this time of night."

"She went out on a date with a customer."

Fright showed in Irma's eyes but was quickly hidden from me.

I added, "Floring figured Georgia would give him the slip pretty fast."

It made her feel better but no friendlier. "Well, she isn't home yet. So I'm afraid . . ."

"I'd like to wait for her. It's important."

She stared at me as though my request confused her. "Wait? Here?"

"You can phone Floring about it. If I worry you."

Irma thought about it, finally shrugged. "Okay. You can wait. Come in."

I climbed the two steps into a living-dining room. An accordion partition screened the kitchenette at one end. Beyond it, a short, narrow corridor led back to the bedroom and bath.

Irma closed the door and stood looking at me uncertainly, her fists planted on her wide hips. "I was just going to sleep when you knocked. I get up early. I run a driftwood factory."

"I'll be quiet," I promised.

She started to turn away, then stopped and looked back at me. "This *man* Georgia's supposed to know. Who is he?"

"Nimmo Fern. Name mean anything to you?"

"Uh-uh. How does Georgia know him?"

"Maybe they met at Floring's Place. He's a gambler."

Irma frowned, worried and thoughtful. "Well . . . don't keep Georgia up too long when she gets in. She never gets the sleep she needs as it is."

"I'll make it short," I assured her.

Irma nodded abstractly, surveyed me a while longer. Then she muttered, "Well . . . good night." She trudged down the corridor to the rear bedroom; closed the door behind her. I waited for the sound of her locking the door. She did.

I sat on the sofa, took my time lighting a cigarette, and prepared for a wait.

Seven cigarettes later, I was still waiting, and the inside of my mouth was beginning to taste like ashes. I went to the kitchenette, had a long, cool drink of water, and went back to the sofa. Another hour went by. No Georgia McKay. I finished the pack of Luckies, prowled the room in search of more cigarettes. No luck. I went back to the sofa. The weariness of the waiting began to get to me. Finally, I stretched out on the sofa, propping my ankles up on one of the arm rests. After a while I closed my eyes.

When I opened them again, daylight was filtering in through the Venetian blinds.

It was the sound of the trailer door opening and clicking shut that awakened me. I sat up quickly, blinking my eyes open. A tall girl with silver-dyed hair and the shoulders, breasts, and hips of a Venus de Milo stood there, her startled gaze fastened on me.

I rubbed my palms over my sleep-numbed face and stared back at her. She wore a strapless black evening gown cut daringly low across the generous hills of her bosom and tucked tight around her tiny waist. Her features were so beautifully chiseled, with just a touch of sensuality to the flare of her nostrils and curve of her lips, that you almost missed the peculiar dead look of her flat gray eyes.

"Who . . ." she whispered tensely.

"Floring sent me," I told her quickly. "I'm looking for Nimmo Fern. Floring thought you could help me. You *are* Georgia McKay, aren't you?"

She nodded, still not adjusted to my presence there. She flicked a worried glance toward the rear bedroom. "But . . . Irma?"

"She went to sleep." I looked at my watch. It was six thirty in the morning. "We thought you'd be home before this."

"I . . ." Georgia licked her lips, tore her worried gaze from the rear of the trailer, looked back at me. "What do you want with Joe?"

"Joe? It's Nimmo Fern I'm looking for."

"Yeah. But Joe Furman's his real name. He—" She stopped herself. "He in some kind of trouble?"

I shook my head. "I owe him some money, can't find him. Nobody seems to know where he is. Maybe you do?"

Georgia shrugged her magnificent bare shoulders. "I haven't seen him around in about a week."

"Know where he lives?"

"Not now. I know he was at the Raymond Arms a couple of months ago. But he moved out. I don't know where he's staying now."

"You're the first person I've come across that knows him by any name but Nimmo Fern," I said. "You must know him pretty well."

"He's from my old neighborhood. I hadn't seen him in years. Then he showed up at Floring's Place."

"Where's the old neighborhood?"

"Brooklyn. In Canarsie." Georgia flashed another frightened glance toward the rear of the trailer, brought her voice back down to a whisper. "His old lady lived next door to my father's butcher shop."

"What was his line up in New York?"

"Search me. He was in some kind of racket, I think. But I wouldn't know. Whatever he did, it was in Manhattan. I only saw him around when he came out to visit his old lady sometimes. I was just a kid then."

"What's *your* real name?" I asked her.

"Doris Ploucher. Why?"

"Have you got any idea how I could find him? It's quite a lot of dough I've got for him."

She shook her head, licked her lips nervously. "You'd better go now. I—"

"Know anybody else that might give me a lead to him?" I persisted. "Or any special place he hung out?"

She shook her head again. "I can't help you. I never see him except in Floring's Place. Got no reason to."

"Ever hear him mention a Jules Langley? Or Catleg?"

She thought about it. "Uh-uh. He never talks about anybody he knows or anything he's doing. Just about the old neighborhood, and how'd his old lady look last time I saw her. Things like that. Now, please, I think you'd better—''

She cut off in mid-sentence as the bedroom door opened and Irma came out, wearing her bathrobe and the drugged look of having been awakened from a deep sleep.

She advanced into the living room, her angry eyes sliding past me to fasten on Georgia McKay-Doris Ploucher.

''Where the hell've you been till this hour?'' Irma rasped.

Sick fright distorted Georgia's lovely face. ''I . . . I had to go out with one of Floring's big-money customers,'' she blurted. ''I couldn't shake him till now.''

''Couldn't shake him,'' Irma mimicked nastily. ''You bitch! What *did* you do with him?''

''Nothing! I swear it, Irma. We just went from bar to bar drinking. I never met a man that could drink so much without falling down.''

''So you finally had to go to bed with him!'' Irma snarled.

''No, honest. He kept trying. But each bar we left, I steered him into the next one. Till we got to Murray's. That's got a back door beside the ladies' room. That's how I was finally able to give him the slip. I ran down the alley and caught a cab and—''

''Liar!'' Irma sobbed. Tears began to stream down her cheeks. ''Lying little tramp!'' She drew her arm back and slapped Georgia full-handed across the face. The sound of the slap was very loud in the confines of the trailer. It rocked Georgia's head back. A little hurt scream came through her clenched teeth. She clasped her cheeks in her hands and began to cry.

''I didn't *do* anything,'' she whimpered brokenly. ''Irma . . . you know I wouldn't. . . . Can't you ever trust me?''

''How *can* I?'' Irma choked out. ''I can't stand it when you—''

Georgia suddenly threw her arms around Irma. That's the way they were, still weeping, when I crossed the room and went out, closing the trailer door on their little scene of domestic strife. Like most I get to witness, it was an-

other second-act scene. I could guess at the beginnings of
this particular drama. I didn't want to speculate on its
probable end.

It was half past four that Wednesday afternoon when I
pulled up the Olds at the curb in front of the Kosterman
construction plant in Mayport.

I'd spent most of the day trying to track down the elu-
sive Nimmo Fern, starting with the Raymond Arms apart-
ments on Miami Beach, the place Georgia McKay had
mentioned. He'd moved out two months before. I managed to trail him from there to a motel where he'd stayed
a week, and from there to one of the best hotels on Collins
Avenue, where he'd stayed two weeks. But I couldn't find
out where he'd moved to from there.

That accounted for my morning. After lunch, I began
waking up various acquaintances of mine in the gambling
profession. Some of them knew Nimmo Fern. None knew
him as Joe Furman. Nobody knew where to find him.

So I finally drove up to Mayport to tackle it from the
other end.

Jules Langley had been from New York. So was Nimmo
Fern.

I knew one other person in this tangle from New York.
Rita Kosterman.

That, by itself, could be just a coincidence. But everything else I knew fitted it too well.

Rudolph Kosterman. Rita. Diana. Darrell Pines. One of
them was the link to Jules Langley and Nimmo Fern.

All four had been present when I'd brought Diana home
from her binge. Any one of them might have noticed that
her daisy pin was missing and phoned Langley about it,
setting him on me. But the most likely person was Rita;
she'd undressed Diana and put her to bed.

Either Diana or Rita would have been best able to slip
the jewels to Langley without their being missed. But
Diana had finally told her father about the missing pin so
he could notify the insurance company. Rita had been
against her doing that, first and last.

It was Rita—after Langley and Oscar had failed to find the pin on me or my property—who had suggested Diana come to me with an offer for its return.

And it was Rita who had reacted so strongly to Nimmo Fern when Anne Archer brought him to the beach party on Kosterman's estate. That had been about four months ago. Hendrik Ruyter had begun substituting the phony stones in the Kosterman jewels about one month after that.

It could still be one of the other three: Kosterman, Diana, Pines. But first I'd find out what I could come up with, digging into Rita's past. . . .

Kosterman kept me twiddling my thumbs in his waiting room for five minutes before his secretary ushered me into his office. Unlike his home, his office was small and plainly furnished—it suited him better. It might have been the office of one of his draftsmen. Blueprints and architects' drawings were scattered on his desk, on a long metal table by the windows, and tacked to the walls.

He sat behind his desk anxiously till his secretary went out, shutting the door quietly behind her. "I'm sorry I kept you waiting," he said. "I was on the phone with a contractor. He wouldn't stop talking till I knew all his troubles."

"S'all right," I told him, and sat in a chair beside his desk.

"I understand the police gave you a bad time," Kosterman said.

"I've had worse. How about you?"

"Russ Patrick, our chief of police here in Mayport, handled them for me."

"So I heard."

Kosterman's massive shoulders hunched forward. "You've got some news for me?"

"Not yet. What was your wife's maiden name?"

His jaws tightened. Nerves twitched the flesh under his eyes. "Nielsen," he said softly. "Rita Nielsen. You think Rita was the one who . . ."

"I want to find out, that's all. She told me she met you in a bar in New York. Remember the name of the place?"

"It was the cocktail lounge in my hotel. The Columbia Towers on Central Park South."

"That's a help . . . your being able to remember that."

"Why?" he demanded, holding back anger.

"You hired me to find out who was responsible for stealing the gems, remember?"

"Yes, but . . . I thought it might be Darrell. He wants to start a firm of his own, to feel independent of me. Or Diana—she's always wanting to give money to her mother and Boyd."

"You think your daughter or Pines would be more likely to steal?"

"I didn't think any of us would," Kosterman said heavily. "But someone apparently did."

"Uh-huh. Someone."

"But not Rita." He tried to say it emphatically, but there was pain and fear in his voice.

"Why not?" I asked him.

"She wouldn't have to. I give her all the money she needs or wants. Which isn't much. Her tastes are simple. She has her own personal checking account. Whenever she wants more money put in it, she tells me. I put it in. No questions asked."

"Those missing gems are worth more than a hundred thousand bucks," I pointed out. "Suppose she'd asked you for that much?"

"She'd have gotten it."

"No questions asked?"

His eyes dropped to his hands. He picked up a letter opener and slowly bent it into the shape of a horseshoe. Then he straightened it with a savage jerk.

"You think it was Rita," he muttered, half to himself.

"I didn't say that. I said I'm going to find out."

"Have you talked to her about it?"

"I tried to get her on the phone several times today," I told him. "She's not home."

Kosterman nodded slowly. "That's right. I remember now. She told me this morning she was going to do some shopping in Palm Beach."

"Any idea when she'll be back home?"

"She'll be coming here." He glanced at his watch. "In about fifteen minutes to pick me up in her car. She always does. We've got enough cars for all of us, but Rita likes driving me to and from work." He paused, then added unhappily, "She says it helps make her feel like a very proper suburban wife."

I stood up. "That gives me fifteen minutes I need. Got a phone I can use for a private long-distance call?"

Kosterman got up slowly from behind his desk. He had aged since I'd entered the office. "Use mine here," he said wearily. "I've got to make my last tour of the plant for the day anyhow."

"I'm going to need some outside help," I told him. "It'll cost you."

"Of course," he mumbled. "Whatever you think best. Just remember. Whatever you find out, I want it kept in the family."

He went out, walking slowly, heavily.

I sat on the edge of his desk, picked up the phone, and put a call through to Nate Feldman, a New York private detective whom I'd dealt with before.

"Tony?" Feldman said when he came on the phone. "Good to hear from you again. How's the weather down there in Florida?"

"Balmy."

"You lucky bastard. I'm chilled to the bone up here. It's been taking turns snowing, raining, and sleeting outside. How's the fishing?"

"Not doing much of it at the moment."

"Hearing your voice," Feldman said sadly, "makes me want to close shop for a couple of weeks, come down there and go out with you on that boat. Get a tan, some fishing, and my good nature back."

"Any time, Nate," I told him. "But first I've got a job for you. Got time to handle it?"

"For love or money?"

"Money."

"You got the money, I got the time. I'm listening."

"There's some people I want you to check on. First, a woman named Rita Nielsen. Four years ago, my client met her in the cocktail lounge of the Columbia Towers on Central Park South. Maybe she hung out there regularly. Maybe somebody there remembers her." I described Rita Kosterman to him. "That isn't much to go on, I know. But that's all I have right now on her. If I get more, I'll let you know."

"Check," Feldman said. "How about the others?"

"Jules Langley. He had a jewelry store near Times Square till a year and a half ago. He had to skip town because the law was starting to lean on him. So the cops'll have some info on him."

"Jules Langley," Feldman said. "Anybody else?"

"Nimmo Fern. That's what he calls himself down here. He's some kind of gambler. His real name's Joe Furman. He's from the Canarsie section of Brooklyn. His mother still lives there or did. Next door to a butcher named Ploucher. That's all I've got for you."

"Okay. What do you want?"

"I want to know if any one of those three was connected in any way with one of the others," I told him. "That's one thing. And I'd like whatever background you can get me on Rita Nielsen and Joe Furman, the guy that now calls himself Nimmo Fern. Third, try like hell to find out Fern's present address down here in the Miami area. He's had a lot of them. I have to find him now. His mother'd be most likely to know if she's still alive. Apparently he kept in touch with her."

"That it?"

"One more thing. See if you can turn up anything about a guy named Catleg. That's all I know about him."

"Sounds like a full week's work. When do you need it?"

"Yesterday. I'll call you tomorrow and see what you have by then."

"That means I won't be doing much sleeping tonight. Again."

"Figure out a fee that'll make up for it," I told him. "My client can afford it."

After hanging up the phone, I sat for a while smoking and guessing at the best approach to pumping some truth out of Rita Kosterman.

The cigarette tasted lousy. I'd been smoking too many of them. It struck me that when I was out on the water with the boat, I never smoked at all.

Promptly at five P.M., Kosterman and I left the front building of his construction company. His wife, Rita, was waiting for him behind the wheel of a bronze-trimmed cream Fiat convertible, parked at the curb in front of my Olds. It made my sedan look like a shabby sufferer from elephantiasis. There were several large, gaily wrapped packages in the rear seat of the Fiat with Palm Beach store labels on them. Rita Kosterman was wearing peach-colored slacks and an off-white blouse. Her eyes widened when she saw me with her husband. I noted the way her hands clenched tighter on the wheel as we came across the pavement toward her.

"Dear," Kosterman told her gently, "Rome has some questions he wants to ask you."

"Does he?" she said tensely. She didn't look at me.

"Yes," Kosterman said. "He . . ." He glanced uncomfortably at me. "I'll tell you what, Rome. Suppose you follow us home in your car. We'll be able to talk better there."

I said "Sure" and started for my Olds as Kosterman stepped off the curb and walked around the front of the Fiat to get in the other side.

He was out in the street when I noticed the late-model blue Ford sedan parked directly across the street, its motor idling.

What drew my attention to it was the loud snap of its brake being released. There was a man behind the wheel in the Ford, wearing a hat pulled low on his forehead. The shadow from its brim blurred the outlines of his face. I only glanced in his direction. I was about to look away again when the rays of the lowering sun glinted on the barrel of the revolver he was raising above the sill of his open car window.

I screamed, "Kosterman! Drop!" as I spun and snatched under my jacket for my own gun.

Kosterman, startled, whirled to look in my direction as the gun in the hand of the man across the street coughed. The bullet jarred into Kosterman, hurling him against the side of the Fiat windshield. His big body twisted slowly, his knees buckling and his torso folding over the hood of the Fiat.

By then I had my .38 out. I squeezed the trigger as I brought the gun up. It roared as it bucked against the heel of my hand. The slug missed the man in the Ford and crashed through the glass of the windshield in front of him. I hadn't taken the time for dead aim, triggering off that first snap-shot as fast as I could to frighten him from trying another shot.

It worked. The gun dropped below the Ford window sill. I saw him grab the steering wheel with both hands as his motor roared, and he rocketed the car away from the curb down the street.

I fired after it twice, aiming more carefully this time. The bullets shattered the rear window, but they didn't get to the driver. Before I could try again, the Ford careened around the corner and vanished from sight.

I sprinted to where Kosterman lay in the street beside the Fiat's front tire. Rita knelt beside him, staring down at his unconscious face.

She wasn't touching him. She wasn't crying. She wasn't screaming.

She looked as if there was a balloon blowing up inside her that at any second was going to burst.

Chapter 16

We waited in the white corridor outside the operating room of the Mayport Hospital. Diana Pines sat on a wooden bench with her worried husband, clutching his hand and crying softly, her head lowered. Rita Kosterman stood leaning against the wall, staring blank faced at a spot on the opposite wall just above my head. A little bit apart from us, one of the police chief's deputies paced nervously, looking uncomfortable as the waiting stretched.

That was the way we were when Russ Patrick, the Mayport chief of police, came back out of the operating-room door, his grim face perspiring. Patrick was tall and hardlean and young for his job, not more than thirty. But he looked tough enough and smart enough for a city the size of Mayport. He wore khaki trousers and jacket and an ordinary business hat. His badge of office was pinned to his lapel.

Diana and Pines looked up quickly, anxiously, as Patrick came through the swinging door. Rita turned her face to look at him; otherwise, neither her position nor her expression changed.

Diana, tears staining her face, blurted, "Russ, is he . . ."

"Doc Andrews is taking out the slug now. He says he'll be all right. It got him in the shoulder. Lucky he moved when he did or I guess it would've broken his spine."

Diana moaned and lowered her face to her hands. Her husband put his arm around her shoulders and murmured, "Don't, honey. He'll be all right, just like the doctor says.

144

It's only a shoulder wound. Hell, I got a lot worse than that in the war, and I'm still around and healthy enough to make trouble for you.''

Chief Patrick looked at me, then at Rita Kosterman. "Okay, now. Did either of you see enough of the guy that shot him to give me a description?"

I shook my head.

Rita had gone back to staring blankly at the opposite wall. Her whispered ''no'' didn't move her lips.

Patrick sighed. "How about the car?"

Rita spoke first in a low, even monotone, "Blue sedan. New."

Patrick looked at me. I nodded. "Ford two-door hard-top. The Galaxie Club Victoria model."

"Get the license number?"

I glanced at Rita, waiting to hear what she'd say.

She surprised me: "I didn't get all of it. I think it started with SJ-4."

"That's right," I told Patrick. "The rest of it's 61."

Patrick turned to his waiting deputy. "Well? What're you standing there for? *You* should've got that."

The deputy said defensively: "I was waiting for you. I figured. . . ."

"For chrissake stop talking," Patrick snapped at him. "You've got the description and number on the car. Get on it."

The deputy hurried off along the hall and ran down the steps.

Patrick turned back to us. "Okay . . . anybody got any ideas on who'd want to kill a nice guy like Mr. Koster-man?"

Diana shook her head without raising it.

Darrell Pines said, "Hell no. I'll tell you something. Rudy's a rough man to do business with. But even men he'd outsmarted on a contract or gotten a job away from couldn't stay sore at him. He's that kind of guy. Everybody likes him."

"Somebody doesn't," Patrick stated. He looked at Rita.

"Mrs. Kosterman? Any idea? Any personal enemy, maybe?"

Rita Kosterman went on staring at the wall above my head. Something unpleasant flickered in her eyes. But she didn't answer him.

Patrick frowned and turned to me. "Well?"

"I've got some ideas," I told him. "Nothing definite. And I don't want to say anything till I talk to Kosterman when he comes out of it."

"He may not be in any shape to talk to you today."

"He will be," I said. "It's only his shoulder. He's healthy and built solid. And he'll be wanting to talk to me as soon as he comes around."

"Oh?" Patrick eyed me, looking like he didn't know whether to be sore about it or not. Finally he just said: "I've been hearing a lot about you the past couple of days. From the boys down in Miami."

"Mostly bad I imagine."

"*All* bad. They're pretty sore at you."

"I don't imagine they like you very much, either," I said.

Patrick nodded. "Not much. But that's no skin off my nose. They figure I'm just a hick cop and I figure to hell with 'em. This is my bailiwick. They can't bother me any. But with you it's different. You got to live with 'em. You better come up out of all this smelling mighty sweet and bringing 'em a present."

"I don't know how I'll be smelling by then," I said, "but I figure on having that present for them."

"Yeah?" Patrick shrugged, took a pipe from his jacket pocket, and began stuffing tobacco into it. "This is getting too complicated for me. Sometimes I wish I was back in the MP's."

Ten minutes later Dr. Andrews came out of the operating room. Diana jumped up off the bench, but Rita got to him first. She seized his white jacket with the fingers of both hands as if she were going to tear it off him. "How is he?" she whispered harshly. "Will he . . ."

Dr. Andrews gave her his best bedside-manner smile

and patted her arm. "He's going to be just fine, Mrs. Kosterman. I got the bullet out. It didn't even break the bone. Of course there's shock and loss of blood. But we've given him a transfusion and . . . well, just take my word for it. Your husband is going to be all right. By tomorrow he'll probably be sitting up and demanding rare steaks."

Rita slumped back against the wall, squeezing her eyes tightly shut. I saw it was requiring willpower to keep her knees from buckling.

Diana, looking as though a heavy weight had been removed from her, asked the doctor, "Can we go in and see him now?"

"Not yet. He's just coming out of the anesthetic. I'll let you know when."

"I want that bullet," Patrick told him.

"I have it for you, inside." The two of them went into the operating room, came back out a minute later. Patrick had the slug in a white envelope. He hurried off down the corridor. The doctor went in the opposite direction, toward the private rooms.

Five minutes later Patrick returned. "I sent the slug over to the state police lab," he told me. "Looked like a .38 to me. That mean anything special to you?"

I shook my head. But I thought about the .38 slug that had killed Turpin.

We waited.

An hour dawdled by. Dr. Andrews reappeared. "Russ," he told the chief of police, "Mr. Kosterman wants to see you."

Patrick gave me a pleased grin. "Wise guy."

Rita asked Dr. Andrews, "Rudy's conscious? He *is* going to be all right?"

Dr. Andrews smiled at her soothingly. "Of course. Just as I told you. You'll be able to see for yourself, after he talks to Chief Patrick. Come on, Russ."

They went off toward Kosterman's room. I looked at Rita. "Mrs. Kosterman, there were those questions I was going to ask you. Maybe we'd better get them over with now."

"It'll have to wait," she said, meeting my eyes without expression.

"It can't wait much longer," I told her.

"I know," she said. "I know that. Just till I see Rudy."

A couple of minutes later Patrick came back, his face grim again. He looked at me. "You win. I'm just a hick cop who does what I'm told. He wants to see *you*."

Dr. Andrews was waiting for me outside Kosterman's room. "Make it short," he said. "He's not that strong yet, and his family will want to see him next."

I nodded and went in. Kosterman's nurse closed the door as she went out, leaving me alone with him. The smell of ether spiced the air in the room. Kosterman rolled his head slowly toward me in the hollow of his pillow. His face was gaunt, its flesh collapsed in on the bone structure. His eyes were only half open but quite clear as they focused on me. He raised one limp hand a few inches off the top sheet in a weak greeting.

"Almost got me," he said in a very small voice that revealed more than anything else how completely he'd been drained of strength. "That was a surprise."

"To me, too," I admitted. "I never guessed there'd be an attempt on your life. I still don't know the why of it. Maybe you do."

"I can't think of any reason," Kosterman said.

"There's money," I said. "Money's always a strong reason for murder."

"Money," he repeated. "Yes . . . I used to think money would solve all my problems. But it just makes more of them. . . . I'm scared, Rome. Not for myself."

"Sure. I don't blame you. It makes you wonder about the people closest to you. The ones who'd benefit from your death."

"Yes."

"Well, it's better to know, Mr. Kosterman. Who does get your money when you're dead?"

He rolled his head away from me on the pillow till he was looking toward the drawn blinds of the windows.

It was a while before he answered: "Rita . . . Oh, God!"

"Just your wife? How about your daughter? Your son-in-law?"

"Darrell doesn't get anything except through Diana. Of course I expected Rita would want him to take over as manager of my businesses. Diana—by the terms of my will the sum left to her will be doled out to her in monthly amounts until Rita's death. To prevent her from giving any large sum to her mother and Boyd."

"Your wife gets the rest? Everything?"

"Everything . . . the insurance, control of my businesses. Everything."

He looked at me again, and now his eyes were wide open. "Rome, I instructed Patrick not to let any other police agency touch this case. Whatever he finds out, he'll report it to me before taking any action on it. And I've told him to work closely with you. That you know best what I want. You do, don't you?"

"Yeah," I said. "Keep it in the family . . . if I can."

"I promised you a generous bonus if you succeeded in doing that. Now I'll name a definite amount. Five thousand dollars. Is that enough? Or . . ."

"It's enough if I can do it. If it can't be done, going higher won't help."

The door opened. Dr. Andrews looked in. "Mr. Rome . . ." he warned.

"I'm leaving now," I told him.

"Rome . . ." Kosterman whispered. "Please . . . *try*."

I said "Yeah" and went out.

Diana and Pines were still on the bench waiting where I'd left them.

Rita Kosterman was nowhere in sight.

Pines rose from the bench. "Well, do *we* get to see him now?"

"Uh-huh. Where's Mrs. Kosterman?"

"She went out for a breath of fresh air. Probably be back any minute."

I hurried off along the hall and ran down the steps to

the hospital entrance. Outside, I looked around for Rita. She wasn't there. Neither was her cream-and-bronze Fiat.

Chief Patrick was in his car at the corner with the door open, talking over his radio-telephone. He hung it on the hook as I leaned in the open door.

"Nothing on that blue Ford yet," he told me. "But there will be. I notified the state police to be on the look-out for it before Kosterman gave me the word to keep it between us."

"Did you see Mrs. Kosterman come out of the hospital?" I asked him.

"Yeah. Said she was going home to get some rest. Guess seeing her husband that way on that hospital bed finished her."

"She *didn't* see him," I told Patrick.

"Oh?" His eyes narrowed. "You think she's the one behind the shooting? And now she's scared and making a run for it?"

"If she is she couldn't get far in that foreign car without being spotted and caught."

"Not by me she won't be," Patrick said, with just a tinge of bitterness. "And I'm not sending out any calls to pick her up. Kosterman gave me my orders. Protect his family even if I have to smother this whole case to do it. And work with you to make sure it's done right."

"Kosterman make the law around here?"

"I've got a big house, a wife who likes good clothes, and three kids to raise," Patrick said. "This is a nice, solid job. With a sweet retirement pension—if I last long enough. I buck Kosterman, and I won't even be considered as a candidate for re-election. That's the way it is."

"I thought you might resent my butting in."

Patrick shrugged. "Not in this case. What the hell, Kosterman's the one got shot. If *he* doesn't want the guilty party prosecuted, why should I care?"

We gave Rita Kosterman ten more minutes to get home, if that was really where she'd gone. Then we went into the hospital receiving room to call the Kosterman estate.

"I'm just doing this out of curiosity," Patrick warned

me as we went in. "If she's skipped, I'm not going to do anything about it. That'll be Kosterman's worry."

I stood by the phone booth as he put through the call. He got the Kosterman butler.

"This is Chief Patrick," he said into the phone. "Is Mrs. Kosterman there?" He listened, said, "Hold on a minute," and looked at me. "She's been—and gone. Left the Fiat and drove away in a black Buick. Guess she figured the Buick'd be harder to find."

"Let me talk to him," I asked Patrick.

He slid out of the booth after telling the butler he was putting his assistant on. I got in the booth and spoke into the phone: "Did Mrs. Kosterman take anything with her when she left? Suitcases? A change of clothes, anything like that?"

"No," the butler said. "No suitcase."

I heard the hesitation in his voice. "What *did* she take?"

"Well . . . she . . . I always keep a loaded revolver in my room just in case. She asked me for it. I gave it to her."

My silence scared him. "Was . . . did I make a mistake?"

"Don't worry about it," I told him. "You've got lots of company."

Chapter 17

I WAS SITTING IN PATRICK'S CAR WITH HIM WHEN THE state troopers' report on the blue Ford with the license number SJ-461 came over the police radio.

The car from which Kosterman had been shot belonged to a druggist in Brookville, a town ten miles south of Mayport. The druggist had reported it stolen on Sunday night.

"Well, that's that," Chief Patrick growled. "Our would-be killer figured somebody might get his license number. So he used a stolen car. We'll find it all right in the weeds off some back road. But he won't be in it. He'll be far away in his own car. Which leaves us nowhere. No way to trace him. We don't even have a description of him. And we can't find him the logical way through whoever he was working for. Because even if Mrs. Kosterman hadn't skipped, Kosterman doesn't want pressure put on his family. Ah, to hell with the whole damn thing."

"Interesting," I commented. "The fact that the Ford was stolen Sunday night. And this is Wednesday."

"So?"

"Sounds like our man's a professional."

Patrick turned his head and gave me his full attention then. "Keep talking."

"The real pro—the experienced killer-for-hire—works it that way. Steals a car for the job. But not the same day he's going to do the job. Because when a car's stolen a

152

bulletin goes out on it. For a while, its description is fresh in the minds of all the prowl-car cops in the area. Any one of them might spot it before the killer got a chance to do his job—or even *while* he was doing it.''

Patrick began to look thoughtful. I gave him the rest of it: ''The real pro steals a car some days before the day of the killing. Then he finds a drop—a garage for rent. He puts the stolen car there and leaves it while he spends the next few days tailing his victim. He learns his victim's habits and decides on the best place and time to do the kill. And by the time he drives the stolen car out to do the job, its description has faded from the cops' minds. Buy it?''

Patrick nodded slowly. ''Maybe. Could be. Somebody in the family hires a professional killer to knock off Kosterman. The killer steals this Ford in Brookville Sunday night, drives it up around here, and hides it somewhere. Then he tails Kosterman in his own car. Sees Kosterman leaves his plant exactly the same time Monday and Tuesday. Five o'clock. And at that time the street where Mrs. Kosterman picks him up is pretty empty. So that's where and when he tries to kill Kosterman on Wednesday. Today. Only today there was something different there at that time. You. You shot back at him and scared him off before he could put a couple more slugs in Kosterman to make sure he was dead. The killer drives off, leaves the stolen car somewhere, and scrams in his own car.''

Patrick got out his pipe and began cleaning it carefully with a pipe cleaner, seeming to give it his full attention.

''Okay,'' he said negligently. ''I'll buy it. It's as good a guess as anything I've been able to come up with. So, while you're giving me lessons in big-city techniques, what do I do now that I know all that?''

I almost told him. But I stopped myself just in time. I had enough cops peeved with me.

''You can figure that out better than I can,'' I told him. ''That's your department.''

Patrick relaxed a bit. He almost smiled. "I figure the first thing we do is find the garage where our killer stashed the Ford. If we can find somebody who remembers renting a garage for that Ford, maybe he'll be able to give us a description of our killer. With his description, we're in business. If he was tailing Kosterman the past couple of days, he must've been staying somewhere around here. We'll check the hotels, motels, and rooming houses till we find where he was holed up. Maybe he's still there. If he's not . . . we'll see." He looked at me. "Sound right?"

"Sounds perfect," I said. "And you don't need me for any of it. I'm behind time for dinner. If you find out anything you want to tell me, I'll be in that diner down on the corner there."

I got out of his car, hesitated, and looked back in at him. "Just a thought," I said carelessly. "You might check the want ads in all the local weekend papers. Try the private garages that were offered for rent on Saturday and Sunday first."

Then I walked down the street to the diner.

The roast beef was tough and stringy; the mashed potatoes were cold and lumpy. But the meal filled me, and the coffee wasn't bad. I sat in a booth making a slow business of drinking cups of the coffee, while I did some thinking about the time element involved in the shooting of Kosterman.

The Ford the killer had used was stolen Sunday night. So quite likely he'd been hired Saturday or early Sunday.

What had happened over the weekend that might have triggered someone into deciding to kill Kosterman?

Friday night, Diana Pines had passed out drunk in the Moonlite Hotel, Turpin had stolen her daisy pin, and I'd taken her home to the Kosterman estate on The Island. Friday night, Langley and Oscar had searched me, my boat, my car, and my office for that pin, but hadn't found it.

Saturday, Diana had hired me to get her pin back. Saturday, I'd gone to Turpin to brace him about the pin, and

Nimmo Fern had tailed me there and listened through the door. Saturday, I'd followed Diana to the ruined estate where her mother lived with Boyd and Boyd's brother—and from there I'd followed her home. There, I'd had my talk with Kosterman, another talk with Rita, and a run-in with Darrell Pines. Saturday night, I'd returned to my office to find Turpin dead. And someone had left my office with Turpin's .45 slug in him.

I racked my brains, going over and over those events. Among them something had happened that had caused someone to want Kosterman dead. I had the feeling the answer was right there, waiting for me to reach out and grab it. But each time I thought I almost had it, it slipped away from me.

I'd been in the diner for less than an hour when Chief Patrick came in, grinning.

He ordered a container of coffee to go, and told me: "Come out to the car. I'm expecting a radio call."

We left the diner together, Patrick carrying his coffee. It had grown dark out. We got into the front seat of his car. The police radio was on, crackling with static and terse messages that didn't concern us.

Patrick peeled the lid off his container and tasted the coffee. "Too hot," he muttered, and began blowing on it.

"Come on," I snapped. "Give."

He laughed, pleased with himself. "We found the garage. It's one of five that were listed for rent in the *Mayport Sunday News*. Attached to a house on the outskirts of the township. The man who owns the house got a phone call late Sunday night from a guy who wanted to know if he'd rented the garage yet. He hadn't. So the guy brought his car around, rented the garage for a month, put the car in it. The guy didn't come back for it Monday or Tuesday. But he did today. Around four in the afternoon. Drove off and hasn't come back yet."

"He won't," I said. "The owner of this garage get the license number?"

"No. But it was a blue Ford. New. And the time element fits like a glove."

"What kind of description of the man were you able to get?"

"You told me the shooter had a hat on," Patrick said. "What color?"

"He was wearing a brown hat."

"So was the man that rented this garage. And a tan summer-weight raincoat. I figure he wore that raincoat so nobody'd see the kind of clothes he had on underneath. Then after he shoots Kosterman, he ditches the stolen Ford, takes off the raincoat and hat, gets into his own car, and goes his merry way."

I nodded. "A real pro. Any more to the description? Outside of his clothes?"

"Uh-huh. A short, skinny man. Walks with a pronounced limp. And he's got a crooked nose. Looks like it was busted, the tip of it turned to one side, like."

I just sat there for a moment, looking at him, remembering the man who had bumped into me when I was tailing Nimmo from Turpin's hotel. Some of the loose ends began tying themselves together for me. I had a sense of things coming full circle.

"With that good a description," I said absently, my mind on other matters, "you've got a real chance of finding his trail."

"We're on it now. I've got every available man out checking him down. Also, I asked the sheriff to have his men look for him in places outside the township. Didn't tell him why, just that I want the guy for questioning." Patrick nodded at the crackling radio speaker. "I'll get called soon as anybody finds any trace of our killer."

"Try checking with the state troopers," I said. "They might have a record on him."

"I already did," Patrick told me, looking pleased with himself again. "And they do. Or anyway, it sounds like the same man. A gun for hire, though they've never been able to prove any killings against him. Works all over Florida. Got a string of aliases as long as your curiosity. Jim MacDonald, Harry Lye, Joe Bailey . . .''

"Calls himself Catleg, lately."

Patrick gave me a sharp look of surprise. "You know him?"

"I think so. He bumped into me last Saturday. *Not* by accident."

"Come on," Patrick snapped impatiently. *"Give."*

"That's all I've got that could help you," I told him.

He glared at me, finally shrugged. "Okay, play it cagey. Anyway, the state cops've been looking for him the past six months. Ever since he shot and killed a gas-station owner in Miami. Seems a small bunch of extortionists was trying to make the independent gas-station owners pay protection. This one wouldn't pay. He wasn't dead when the cops got to him, though he died an hour later. He gave them a description of the guy who shot him. Sounds just like our killer. Except for the limp. And maybe the gas-station owner gave him that. He said he was expecting trouble, so he was carrying a gun when the killer came for him. He put a bullet in the killer's hip before he went down. The killer managed to stagger back to his car and drive off. But that'd account for the limp easy enough."

"It could," I said. "Do they have any kind of lead to him?"

"Nothing. Not where he is or where he's been. . . . I'd sure like to be the one who gets him. It'll probably turn out he's got a lot of other kills to his record. Turning up a killer like that'd be awful good publicity for me. With something like that under my belt, it wouldn't be so easy for the lousy politicos to boot me out of my job just because I step on somebody's toes."

He didn't look at me as he said it, but we both knew what he meant.

He blew on his coffee again, sipped at it. "That's much better," he murmured, and began to drink it.

The Surf Motel was a row of neat little cabins on a strip of waterway beach. Phelps, the motel owner, was waiting in his office with a Mayport prowl-car cop when I entered with Chief Patrick.

Phelps repeated for us what he'd told the prowl-car cop: A man answering our killer's description had registered into one of the motel cabins Sunday night a few minutes before midnight. Phelps had noticed him particularly because of the limp and because he was wearing a raincoat when it wasn't raining. He'd registered under the name Robert Donald. And he'd signed out that morning at eleven o'clock.

"What kind of car was he driving?" Patrick asked him.

"I didn't see no car," Phelps answered. "He come walking, he left walking."

A real pro.

"What kind of hours did this Donald keep?" Patrick asked.

"Well, I don't have time to just sit around keeping tabs on my customers. But as far as I can tell you . . . let's see . . . Monday morning he must've got up real early. He was gone by the time I got up. Came back sometime between ten and eleven that night. Near as I remember. Maybe he was back in his cabin sometime during the day, but I didn't see him."

"How about Tuesday?"

"Same thing. Gone before I got up in the morning. Back late at night. And then this morning like I told you. He checked out at eleven A.M. You gonna tell me what he did?"

"No," Patrick snapped. "Did he have any visitors?"

Phelps shrugged. "I don't know. Not that I know of."

"Did you notice anything at all about him that might give us a lead to him? Anything he told you, or . . ."

"Well . . ." Phelps said, "last night after he came in he made a phone call. It was almost midnight. That help any?"

Chief Patrick stiffened. "How do you know? Don't your cabins have their own phones?"

"Uh-uh. Haven't put any in yet. Just got this office phone here, and the pay phone outside the door there. He used the pay phone."

"Could you hear what he said over the phone?"

"How could I? I was in here, he was out there."

"Don't you ever eavesdrop?" Patrick demanded.

Phelps reddened. "Hell no! I don't. . . . What do you take me for?"

"You'd be a hero, if you did this time."

Phelps shook his head. "Well, I didn't. Honest. I heard him dropping the coins in, but that's all I heard."

Patrick sighed. "*Big* help."

"Maybe it is," I said. I looked at Phelps. "You said you heard him drop coins in. You mean *coins*? Not just one coin?"

"No. Like I said. I heard a bong, and a couple tinkles, like, and . . . Why?"

Patrick and I looked at each other.

I said, "Long distance."

"Yeah," Patrick breathed happily. "That means there'll be a record of it."

He snatched up the desk phone, used it to call the telephone company. It didn't take him long to get the information he wanted. He hung up and motioned to me. We left the motel office together.

In the darkness outside Patrick told me, "The call went to Miami. The Hotel Blue Bell." He gave me the address. "Miami ain't my territory. But your license is supposed to be good anywhere in the state."

"Lucky me."

"Yeah," he said dryly. "You get to go down there after him."

"Wish me luck."

"You wear a gun," Patrick said. "Take some advice. This killer is nobody to play games with. You spot him— shoot him first and ask the questions after."

"Can't," I told him. "The questions I have to ask him need answers."

Patrick raised and lowered a shoulder. "Do or die for dear old Kosterman."

"I'll be in touch," I said.

"Sure. If I don't hear from you, I'll look for your name in the papers. The obituary column."

Chapter 18

It was one a.m. when I reached Miami.

The Blue Bell was at the bottom of Miami. Not geographically, but in every other way.

It was in hillbilly town, a festering sore of a neighborhood jammed against the railroad freight tracks. It was mostly clapboard shacks, few with inside plumbing, set up on concrete blocks and surrounded by lush, untended eruptions of wild subtropical vegetation. Each shack was home for a dozen or more of the dirt-poor Southern whites who kept trickling down to Miami from the swamps and backwoods hills of the states bordering northern Florida. They brought no sense of law with them—only a rigid code of crude private justice. Shootings and stabbings were so common in hillbilly town, and their survivors so dangerous, that the Miami cops seldom entered it except for a major riot threatening to spill out into neighboring sections. Then they came by the dozen.

The Blue Bell was part of a short block that comprised the best street in the neighborhood. First of all, the street was asphalt, instead of gravel or dirt. And it had pavements. Most of its buildings were gin mills. From each thundered a weird perversion of music—part Western, part hillbilly, part rock 'n' roll, part pure howl of rage; the blending of these parts sounding as if it had been accomplished in a cement mixer.

I got hostile, suspicious glares as I came down the pavement. I wasn't wearing the right uniform, didn't have the right look. The males prowling the street all wore skin-tight Levi's tucked into cowboy boots and gaudy sports shirts unbuttoned to show their bare chests and navels; they sported sideburns and long greasy hair, sullen mouths and vacant eyes. Most of the females were indistinguishable at a quick glance from the males—except that some of them had their shirts partly buttoned. And some wore sleazy dresses made of some material not too far removed from tissue paper.

The sign painted on the stucco wall over the open door-way between two of the gin mills read:

HOTEL
BLUE BELL

The narrow wooden stairway inside was dark. But there was light at the top of it. A naked light bulb dangled at the end of a ceiling electric cord. I made my way up the rickety flight of steps to the glare of the lighted landing. There was a sort of foyer there, just big enough to contain the wooden table with the hotel register book on it, two kitchen chairs, and space to squeeze past to an unlighted corridor of room doors.

No one was there. A pullrope hung by a cardboard sign in which had been printed in pencil: "RING BELL." There was another penciled cardboard sign on the wall: "*NO* Guests Allowed in Rooms After 9 P.M." By hillbilly-town standards that sign—enforced or not—proclaimed the Blue Bell a solid, first-class establishment.

There was a pay phone on the opposite wall. I had a look at the number on its dial. It was the number the killer had called from the Surf Motel in Mayport.

I yanked on the pullrope.

He was quick enough opening the nearest room door and popping out into the corridor. But he did everything after that with a lethargy so deep it could only have been acquired through a lifetime of effort. He was about forty—tall, consumptive, pot-bellied. He had on baggy brown trousers, a green shirt, a threadbare blue jacket. There was a bulge in the right-hand pocket of the jacket. I guessed it was a gun he carried for protection, though in that neighborhood a gun would be about as much help to him as a blunt knitting needle.

He leaned against the corner of the wall next to the table, looking at me sleepily. "You're wrong," he drawled.

"About what?"

"I see you looking at my pocket. You think maybe I can't get the gun out before you jump me. But I can."

"Why should I jump you?"

He shrugged in slow motion. "Maybe you're thinkin' of holding me up, maybe."

I stared at him. "Is there anything around here worth stealing?"

"No . . . but maybe you wouldn't know that."

"I might guess it."

He began cleaning his grimy fingernails with a toothpick. "Well . . . one thing I know. You didn't come up here looking for a room."

"No? How much are the rooms?"

"Dollar a day. But you don't want one. Not you."

"Any of the rooms have a phone?"

He nodded at the pay phone on the wall. "We're lucky we still got that one. Next time some damn fool drunk rips it outa the wall, the phone company ain't gonna put it back."

"Who answers the phone when it rings?"

"Me."

"Suppose you're not here?"

He finished cleaning his nails with the toothpick. They didn't look any cleaner. He began using the toothpick on his teeth. "I'm *always* here. This is *my* hotel."

"Nice place you've got here."

His eyebrows inched upward. "Maybe you've seen better."

"I've seen worse, too." I took out a five-dollar bill, fanned it across my fingers. "A long-distance call came in here last night from Mayport. About midnight. Who was it for?''

He contemplated the five, scratching his ear with the toothpick. I gave him time. He took it.

Finally my patience ran thin. I slapped my palms together, loudly, concealing the fiver between them.

His eyes widened in astonishment, as though I'd performed a feat of magic. "Hey . . ." he murmured unhappily.

I opened my hands and showed him the five-dollar bill again. "The call," I said.

"Well, now . . . why? Who're you?''

I started to close my hands, slowly this time, making the bill vanish an inch at a time.

The toothpick snapped between his fingers. "Make it ten?''

"I'm thinking of dropping it to two-fifty.''

The five was almost out of sight between my closing hands. He hated to see it go.

"Sally Bullock," he said. "The call was for her.''

I opened my hands and lowered them, letting the five dangle from a thumb and forefinger. "Sally Bullock. She have a room here?''

"Naw. I don't let in that kind. This guy asked me to get her from the joint next door. The Gulch. Phone company took their phone out. So I got her.''

"Know who the man on the phone was?''

He shook his head.

"Who's this Sally Bullock?''

He did his slow-motion shrug. "A girl. Used to see her around a lot. Till she moved away. Now she only comes around once in a while. Dresses nice now.''

"What did you mean when you said she was *that kind*?''

"You know. A junkie. I don't let 'em in here ever. They're worse'n drunks. A junkie'll kill you for the price of a shot. Pretty thing though.''

"You said she moved away. Where'd she move?''

"Dunno.''

"She next door now?''

"Wouldn't know. Ain't been in The Gulch tonight."

"Did you hear what she said over the phone here?"

He pursed his lips thoughtfully. "That oughta cost you extra."

"You haven't earned the five yet."

"Suppose I lie to you?"

I smiled at him. "What do you think I'd do about it when I found out?"

"I carry a gun," he reminded me.

"So do I."

He sighed. "It figures." He yawned. "She didn't say much. Just come to the phone and said 'Hello.' Then she said. 'When?' and 'I'll be waiting.' Then she hung up and left." He eyed the bill in my hand. "The five?"

"One more thing." I described the man who'd shot at Kosterman—his limp, the crooked nose. "Ring a bell?"

He wagged his head from one side to the other. "Don't know anybody like that. Know lots of busted noses. Some limps. Not the two of 'em together."

I gave him the bill. He took it and stuck it in his pocket like it didn't mean much to him.

"Anything else I ought to know?" I asked him.

"What d'you want from me? You got your five's worth."

"Sure," I said. I got another five-dollar bill from my pocket and stuck it in his hand. "This is for nothing. Just because I like your face."

His jaw sagged. After the way I'd squeezed him for the first five, my sudden generosity shocked him.

I said, "So long" and turned to go. But I didn't hurry it.

"Wait," he said.

I looked back at him.

"Folks in The Gulch don't like strangers wanderin' in," he told me slowly. "It's kind of a club. You know? Get in and out fastlike if you want to come out in one piece."

I said, "Thanks."

He frowned and went on fingering the five, looking guilty about having it, wanting to earn it.

"This's real generous of you," he murmured.

"It's not my money," I told him. "Expense account."

"Yeah?" He frowned some more, then stuck the five in his pocket to warm the other one. "I'll tell you what. If Sally Bullock ain't there . . . there's a gal hangs out in The Gulch used to be thick with her when Sal worked there as a barmaid. Name's Fat Candy. Maybe she knows where Sally Bullock'd be. You make out like you want her company for an hour and get her the hell outa there. Won't none of the boys stand in the way of her makin' some quick dough."

I told him thanks again and went down the narrow stairway. Something new had been added at the bottom of the steps. An old wino was stretched out asleep on the pavement, snoring alarmingly. I stepped over him and turned right, into The Gulch.

It was a plain, square room with walls that couldn't remember their last whitewash. The cleanest object in the room was the jukebox in one corner blasting out a hillbilly-rock number at full volume. The wooden bar along one wall and the battered tables and chairs scattered about were crowded. Drunken laughter and shouting competed with the jukebox, the sounds of the men blending into the general noise level, the shriller voices of the women biting through it. The men were all ages, but the women, except for a couple of ancient hags sharing a bottle of wine at the bar, were young; some couldn't have been more than thirteen.

By the time I'd gotten three steps inside The Gulch, only the racket from the juke filled the room. If King Kong had walked in there, he couldn't have gotten more of a reaction than I was getting. Everybody shut up and craned their heads to look at me. Ugly stares clawed and beat at me as I made my way to the bar. The place was frozen like a movie in which part of the sound is suddenly cut off and the reel stops turning.

There was a little space at the bar—between the two wine-drinking hags and a grizzled old man with a three-day growth of gray whiskers stained with tobacco juice. He had one hand up under the shirt of a smirking fifteen-year-old girl, the other hand wrapped around a beer bottle. As I eased against the bar, he let go of the girl and shifted his grip to the neck of his beer bottle, eying me with hot suspicion. He didn't bother me too much. It was keeping my back to the rest of them in that room that gave me the jittery feeling.

A tall, skinny barmaid in tight Levi's and a cowboy shirt planted herself across the bar from me, her gaze expressionless.

"Sally Bullock around?" I asked her.

"I don't know you," she stated flatly.

"My misfortune. I'm looking for Sally Bullock."

"She ain't here tonight."

A nasal voice spoke from behind my right shoulder: "Wha' the hell *you* want 'round here?"

I turned my head. The voice belonged to a teen-age boy with a brutish face, stocky build, and Marlon Brando slouch. An empty wine bottle dangled from his hand.

I shifted my stance so I could look at him and the barmaid at the same time. "How about Fat Candy?" I asked her.

She glanced away down the bar. "Hey! Fat Candy! Guy here wantsa see you."

At the end of the bar, a girl disengaged from a man's arms and looked our way. The barmaid pointed at me. "Him."

Fat Candy strolled toward me, blank faced. She fitted the first part of her name, at least. She wore a tight skirt and a red sweater. The sweater might have been big enough for Jane Russell, but it was way too small for Fat Candy. The man who'd been clutching her lumbered behind her. He had the walk and build of a full-grown rhino.

"Y'want me?" Fat Candy demanded as she reached me.

"Sally Bullock's a friend of mine," I told her. "So're you from what she says. She told me a lot about you."

"Yeah?" The implied flattery in my look and voice got to her. She showed the tip of her pink tongue between her teeth, raised a slow hand to fluff the hair at the back of her neck. "What'd Sal say?"

"Can we go somewhere for a while? Be alone?"

She eyed me calculatingly. "You wanna buy me?"

I glanced around at all those silent, listening faces.

"Something like that," I told Fat Candy.

"For how long?"

"Not long."

"How much?"

"Five?"

"Make it ten," she said automatically.

"All right."

She smiled then, pleased with her financial cunning. "Okay, dear. Come with me."

She turned her back on me, patted the chest of the rhino-sized hillbilly she'd been with. "Stick around, dear," she told him, and strolled toward the rear door of the place.

I followed her, running the gantlet of all those un-friendly eyes. In the darkness outside behind The Gulch, the outlines of a one-room shack bulked. Fat Candy opened the shack door. I followed her inside, feeling my way in the blackness. She struck a match. By its flare I watched her light a kerosene lamp hung on one of the plank walls.

The inside of the shack contained an iron-frame army cot with a bare, dirty mattress, and two wooden chairs. That was all. There were no windows. Just the door. As I shut it, Fat Candy shuffled to the side of the cot and grasped the bottom of her sweater to peel it off.

"Hold on," I said quickly. "It's just some talk I want."

"Huh?" She stared at me, letting go of her sweater. "Talk?" Her face hardened abruptly, her eyes narrowing to slits buttressed by ripe flesh. "You said ten bucks. You try foolin' me and I'll yell for some of my friends. They'll take care of you *good*."

I got out a ten-dollar bill, thankful that it was Koster-man's pocket the money was coming from. I dropped the ten on the mattress. She snatched it up, examined it and raised puzzled eyes to my face.

"It's Sally Bullock I want," I told her. "She said I could find her here. I was supposed to meet her in The Gulch last night. But I wasn't able to make it last night."

"Then you're outa luck," Fat Candy said. "Last night she was here. Tonight she ain't. Since she moved away, she only comes around when her man's gone off someplace. She gets the lonesomes when he's away. I tole her she would moving away. She won't ever find real friends anywhere like she had here."

"Her man? Sally didn't tell me she had a man. Who is he?"

"I dunno. She don't say anything about him. 'Cept about all the dough he's got. She's always showin' off when she comes around. Buyin' drinks for everybody."

"I've got to find her," I said. I dug more bills from my pocket, peeled off five ones, showed them to her. "Tell me where to find her."

She eyed the money, licking her lips greedily. Wheels of thought turned slowly behind her eyes.

"No reason not to tell me," I said. "I'm new down here. I haven't made a contact for the stuff yet. Sally said she'd introduce me to her pusher."

Fat Candy looked at me with more interest. "I can usually spot 'em. But you I didn't figure for a user. What're you on, Charlie or H?"

"Heroin. I need a source of the stuff down here. That's why I have to find Sally Bullock."

"Yeah? You don't look like you need a fix so bad."

"I don't," I told her. "I've still got a couple days' supply. But when that runs out I'll have to head back North. Unless I make a contact down here. I need Sally Bullock to make the contact."

Fat Candy's eyes took in the bills I held again. "I got no idea where Sally lives now," she said. "But you don't need her. *I* know her pusher. He used to peddle around here till he moved on up to where they pay more. He's the one first got Sal hooked a couple years back."

I thought about it. It would have to do. I waved the five

one-dollar bills. "Okay. Give me the contact, and these're yours."

"Make it five more," she said.

"That's too much. You've already got ten from me."

She grinned, eying me out of the depths of her wisdom about dope addicts. "You'll pay it," she stated.

I sighed and got the extra five out. "The contact, first."

"You try renigging after I tell you," Fat Candy warned me, "and you won't get a block away from here. My friends'd catch you and tear you apart."

"You give me Sally Bullock's pusher, I'll give you the ten."

"His name's Vic Rood. He peddles on The Beach. Got an apartment there down near the dog track." She told me the address.

I gave her the bills. She added them to the original ten and folded them into a tight wad. She pulled up her sweater and tucked the wad in a little pocket in the waistband of her skirt.

"You can still have me for another ten," she suggested.

"Not tonight."

She shrugged. "Sure. Or any night. That's the trouble with you junkies. You got a needle fulla junk, you never need anything else."

Chapter 19

THE APARTMENT BUILDING WAS CLOSE TO THE WATER— A long, modern two-story structure bent like a horseshoe around a dark courtyard of flagstone, coconut palms, and the inevitable swimming pool. I followed the inner lanai to the door of Victor Rood's ground-floor apartment at the base of the courtyard. I rang the bell and waited.

In a moment a man's voice came to me through the door panel, "Who?"

"Fat Candy sent me," I answered loudly.

There was silence. Then, "Wait a minute."

I waited almost the full minute before the lock was turned inside. The door opened. About a foot, no more. The man in the opening wore pegged trousers with razor-sharp creases and a beautiful white silk shirt with the initials *VR* embroidered on the pocket in red. He had the face of a bulldog. His eyes were vicious and he smelled bad to me. But then, all dope pushers smell that way. The rot of their victims' souls clings to them.

"Rood?" I asked.

"Yeah. What d'you want?"

His left hand was in plain view, the thumb hooked on his belt. But his right forearm was out of sight behind the partly open door.

"Fat Candy sent me," I repeated. "I need some H. Enough to hold me a few days."

Rood looked me up and down slowly. "I don't know you."

"I'm from Philadelphia. Down here for a few weeks. I've just about run out of the caps I brought with me and—"

"I got no idea what you're talking about, pal."

"Fat Candy said you could help me out."

He shook his head. "Fat Candy's got a fat mouth. She must've been conning you."

He could be right. She might have been.

"Listen," I said, "don't be like that. It's just I'm staying down here a week longer than I'd planned. I only need enough to tide me over three more days. I'll pay you whatever's fair. Hell, I'll pay you more than fair. I'll pay double the usual tab. How's that?" I forced a grin. "Why not? I'm on an expense account. I'll charge it to the company under business entertainment."

I saw the hesitation in his eyes. The temptation of my offer contended with the ingrained caution of his trade. Fat Candy hadn't conned me.

I hit the door with my side, all my weight and the strength of my legs behind the jolting push. The door slammed against his right arm, spinning him away inside. I was through the doorway, kicking the door shut with my heel, by the time he recovered his balance. He twisted back toward me, bringing around the .45 automatic he'd had in his right hand all the time. I caught his right wrist with both hands and twisted. He gritted his teeth to keep from yelling as his fingers sprang open. The .45 thudded to the rug. Rood clubbed his left fist at my face as I yanked him toward me. I took his knuckles on my ear. It hurt, but not enough to stop me from kneeing him in the groin.

A thin cry of horror and pain hissed through his teeth. He bent over his agony and I jerked my knee up into his face, felt teeth breaking against my kneecap.

He sprawled away from me, and I let him go. He went down on his hands and knees spitting jagged tooth ends and blood. He started crawling to his fallen .45. I bent and picked it up before he reached it and dropped it in my jacket pocket. I grabbed him by his silk shirt, lifted him off the floor, and threw him on the living-room sofa.

He sat in the middle of it, hunched over, with blood trickling down his chin, his hands clutching at his hurt. He moaned softly, piteously, his eyes squeezed tightly shut.

I glanced around the place, giving him time to recover. The living room was vast. Its lavish furnishings showed the touch of an excellent interior decorator. I-could see part of a bedroom through an open door; it was more of the same. Rood's apartment would have cost a lot anywhere. On Miami Beach, in season, the rent would be staggering.

But Rood could afford it. I thought of all the men and women and kids who lived in hell so that Rood could live here. People for whom Rood was the only one who could dispense the magic to stave off the claws waiting to rip their insides, the agony ready to eat their brains.

Rood raised his head and looked at me. His eyes killed me a dozen times over in a dozen different ways.

"Why don't you yell?" I suggested. "Somebody'll hear and call the cops. You hid your stock before you opened the door, but I'll bet they'd find it."

He described my ancestry with a few short, blunt words.

I slapped him as hard as I could, knocking him down sideways on the sofa. A tiny scream choked through his clenched teeth. I grabbed him by the hair and jerked him upright again.

"Don't call me names," I told him gently. "That's pressing your luck. I don't like you. Even without knowing you. There's just one line of work I've got a deep hate for. And you're in it. So watch your tongue."

His dazed eyes blinked at me. There was fear in them now.

"Who're you?" he slurred through his broken teeth.

"I'm looking for Sally Bullock. Where do I find her?"

"Who?"

I took his .45 from my pocket, removed the clip, and tossed it away. "No sense my hurting my hands on you," I said, and hefted the gun like a club.

Rood looked at it, then at my eyes. "Wait!" he pleaded raggedly. "Just tell me what this is all about. Just . . ."

I shook my head once. "Sally Bullock," I said tonelessly. "Where do I find her?"

"I don't know," he whispered.

I raised the automatic to hit him.

"I *swear* it!" he bleated, cringing away from me. The begging words tumbled past his bleeding mouth: "I don't know where she lives! It's the truth! She's shacked up with some guy named Catleg, but I don't know where. . . . She comes here for her caps. Why should I care where she goes the rest of the time?"

I lowered the gun just a little. "What's this Catleg look like?"

"Skinny little guy. Bent nose. He limps."

I held back the excitement rising in me. "What's Catleg's first name?"

"How should I know?" Rood muttered. "I only saw him once. With Sal. In one of the joints off Alton. I don't know anything about him." He sat up straighter, some of the fear of being hit again easing up. He pulled out a handkerchief, dabbed at his torn mouth, looked sickly at the blood that came off on the white cloth. "Look," he said weakly, "give me a break. Tell me what it's all about. I got dough. We can square any beef. . . ."

"Nothing to square," I told him. "I'm not the cops. Just keep talking. When was the last time you sold Sally Bullock a supply of heroin?"

"Couple days ago."

"When's she due back here?"

He shrugged. "How should I know?"

I grabbed the front of his shirt and dragged him up off the sofa, letting him feel the cold metal of the gun butt against his cheek. "What you've got now is nothing," I told him softly. "A little dentistry and some false teeth'll fix you up. But if I let you have it with this gun, they'll have to wire your jaw back together. You'll spend a year taking your meals through a glass straw. So no more funny answers."

His hands fumbled weakly at my chest. "Please . . ." he whispered raggedly. "Don't blow your top. I . . . ."

"You know how many caps you sold Sally Bullock last time. You know exactly how deep she's hooked, how many caps a day she needs. You know when she'll run out of 'em and need more." I drew back the automatic, eying his face.

"She's just about due!" Rood gasped out.

I opened my fist and let him fall back to the sofa. "What does that mean? *Exactly.*"

"She should be out of caps by now," Rood mumbled. "I figured she'd of showed up by this time. She's late."

I considered it. I moved to the phone table, keeping an eye on Rood, and looked up the name Catleg in the phonebook. He wasn't in it. I hadn't really thought he would be. That left waiting. There was just one good thing about dope addicts. You could depend on them. They could never move far away from their source of supply. And they had to keep coming back to it for more.

I made Rood get his stock of dope. He'd concealed it up inside his fireplace chimney when I rang the bell and he didn't recognize my voice. It was in a canvas airline bag. I unzippered the bag and glanced inside. There were some sticks of marijuana and some decks of cocaine—called Charlie by users. But most of Rood's stock consisted of capsules of diacetylmorphine, known to the public as heroin, to addicts as Horse or H.

I explained to Rood exactly what I expected of him. Then I let him use the bathroom to clean up. While he was in there, I slipped a fistful of heroin caps out of his bag and hid them under the cushion of his sofa.

After that we waited.

By five fifteen A.M. I was wilting, in spite of the three cups of strong black coffee I'd brewed for myself in Rood's gleaming, modern kitchen. For Miami Beach it wasn't terribly late; but I'd had a full day after a not-too-satisfying sleep on Georgia McKay's trailer sofa.

In the long interval of waiting, a succession of cash-bearing, anxious-eyed supplicants made a pilgrimage to Rood's door—none of them Sally Bullock.

Rood and I played out the same little scene each time a knock sounded at his door.

We played it again for the five-fifteen knock.

I hid in the dark bedroom, with the door open just a couple of inches—enough for me to watch Rood, to shoot him if he made it necessary.

Rood went up to the closed living room door and asked through it, "Who?"

It was a woman's voice that answered through the panel this time. There'd been other women's voices. But this one said, "It's me, Vic. Sally Bullock."

I watched Rood unlock and open the door. The girl who slipped in was small and curvy in flowered toreador pants and a black sweater. Her face was pretty, but what her solid case of the jitters was doing to it wasn't. Her jaws worked feverishly as she chewed at a wad of gum. She wasn't enjoying the gum. She was overdue for her fix; the gum chewing was a pathetically inadequate attempt to pacify her burning nerves.

"You're late for it," Rood said as he shut the door.

"You're telling me," she snapped. "Come on, Vic. I'm in a hurry."

"How much you want this time?"

Sally Bullock dug into a pocket of her toreador pants, fished out a wad of bills, slapped it in Rood's waiting hand. "As much as this'll buy me," she said nervously.

Rood counted the bills, whistled. "This'll buy you a couple weeks' supply."

"That's what I need. I got to get out of town for a while. C'mon. Hurry."

She watched greedily as he counted out capsules of heroin into a small brown grocery-store paper bag.

As he dropped in the last one, she said quickly, "I needa shoot-up right now. Can I use one've your needles?"

There'd been similar requests during my wait. Rood followed my instructions. "In the bathroom," he said. He watched her go to it, but didn't go with her. After she vanished into the bathroom, Rood looked at the bedroom door. He couldn't see me through its narrow, dark opening, but he smiled nervously at me anyway like a bad boy seeking approval from his teacher after he's been whipped into doing the right thing for a change.

When Sally Bullock came out of the bathroom she was a different girl. She moved with a lazy, feline grace. Her eyes were dreamy. Her lips smiled at a private joke.

"Bye now, Vic honey," she murmured. "Won't be seeing you for a couple of weeks."

"Where're you going?" Rood asked, and glanced again in my direction. He wanted to be sure I understood he was trying to help me.

"Away, away," she chanted. "Vacation. My boy friend needs a vacation." She giggled and drifted to the door. Rood opened it and she drifted out with her brown-paper bag full of the devil's groceries.

I came out of the bedroom as Rood shut the door behind her. He turned to me eagerly. "Okay?"

"Fine," I told him. "But look over there at that."

Rood said "Huh?" and turned to look where I was pointing with my left hand.

I raised my right hand with my .38 in it and hit him behind the ear. He was a loose sprawl on the rug when I opened the apartment door and went out.

Sally Bullock was hip-switching her way to the end of the lighted lanai. I moved silently through the dark courtyard, keeping her in sight. She reached the sidewalk and turned left. As I eased up to one of the palms edging the sidewalk, my hand was wrapped around the .38 in my pocket.

She was crossing the street diagonally in the middle of the block, walking quickly. I hesitated in the shadow of the tree. My Olds was parked on my side of the street. If she got into one of the cars parked on the other side, I wanted to be able to reach the Olds quickly enough to be on her tail before she drove out of sight.

But she didn't head for any of the parked cars. She climbed the curb between two of them, hurried off along the opposite pavement, and vanished around the corner. I left the shelter of the palm and hurried across the street the way she had gone, strode up the pavement, and went around the corner after her.

Sally Bullock was jumping into a car as I came around the corner. It was a Chrysler convertible with the top down, facing my way with the motor running. In the light of the street lamp I could see the face of the man behind the wheel plainly. A thin face. A crooked nose. The limping man who'd made me lose Nimmo.

The light that showed him to me showed me to him. And he recognized me.

The Chrysler's motor roared at the same time that I jumped toward the curb dragging the .38 from my pocket. The big car leaped forward. But not away from the curb. He was near enough for me to see the hard set of his face as he twisted the steering wheel. The front tires rammed the curb and mounted it with a bound. The car rocketed straight at me.

The gun in my hands seemed to go off by itself. I saw the spider web of cracks abruptly radiate out from the bullet hole in the windshield, saw his mouth strain wide open as I hurled myself out of the path of the hurtling car.

The side of the fender caught my hip. I was thrown high and spun like a top. I was still spinning through blackness when the rending crash of a couple tons of metal plowing into solid brick reached me. Then the pavement slammed into me and the blackness stopped spinning.

The wail of a distant siren racing nearer corkscrewed me up out of the blackness. My head hurt horribly and there were pains to match it traveling down my leg from my bruised hip. The rest of me just ached. I opened my eyes and found that I was sprawled in the gutter, with two uniformed cops standing over me and a crowd gathered around me and the Chrysler.

The car was across the pavement, with its engine accordioned into the brick wall of the corner building.

The man who'd driven the car—Catleg—was gone.

Sally Bullock hung over the hood like an abandoned rag doll. She'd gone through the windshield into the wall.

What the glass and the brick had done to her made me want to close my eyes again and crawl back into the blackness.

I felt like Typhoid Mary. Wherever I went, I carried death with me. I touched people's lives, and they died. First Turpin. Then Ruyter, Langley, and Oscar. And, almost, Kosterman. Now Sally Bullock. The worst of it was I knew she wasn't the end of it. . . .

Chapter 20

IT WAS FOUR IN THE AFTERNOON WHEN I LEFT THE LOWER Miami Beach police headquarters building. They'd been ready to let me go three hours earlier, but I'd been dead to the world on a cot in the station basement. Sleeping it off.

They'd given me a hard time for a while. Because I was all they had—outside of a dead girl, a smashed car with a bag of narcotics under the front seat, and the fact that the driver of the car had managed to vanish before the first cops arrived on the scene.

So once the police doctor said he'd seen men hurt worse than I was after they'd fallen down a flight of stairs, and pronounced me fit for questioning, the cops had crowded me. I'd had to give them part of the truth: That the driver of the car—a man I knew only as Catleg—had shot my client in Mayport. That I was working with the Mayport chief of police to catch Catleg. That when I'd caught him he'd tried to run me over.

A witness to the accident confirmed the part about the car trying to run me down. And Chief Patrick confirmed by phone that I'd been working for him.

The cops shifted their efforts to trying to find Catleg. They didn't have any success in that direction either. My bullet had hit him. There was blood on the steering wheel, and it wasn't Sally Bullock's. The witness to the smashup had seen Catleg stagger away on foot and said he looked pretty badly hurt. The cops threw a dragnet around the

area and combed it. They didn't comb Catleg out of it.
But an hour after the smashup, a man reported that his
parked car had been stolen, three blocks from where Catleg had driven the Chrysler into the wall.

The Chrysler didn't help either. It was registered to Sally
Bullock. And the address she'd given on her driver's license was a place she hadn't lived in for a year.

Most of these facts came in after I had passed out on
the cot in the basement of the station. Lieutenant Myers,
in charge of the investigation, gave them to me after I rose
from my hours of oblivion.

Myers accompanied me to the station entrance.

"You're limping pretty bad," he commented as I hob-
bled down the hall beside him. "How's it feel?"

"Like it looks. Lousy."

"That's the kind of day this is. Lousy. A day like this
I can do without." Myers sighed theatrically. "A real
nothing day. I got a wrecked car with a bag full of dope
in it. I got a girl that's dead. I got a professional killer—
maybe named Catleg—that I can't find. I got you that I've
got to let go. I should've stayed home sick today. That'd
look better on my record than anything I'm gonna make
out of this case."

"How'd a narcotics arrest do for your record?" I asked
him.

He looked bored. "A user?"

"A pusher. Retail. But big."

He began to look interested. "Ah, now. On a day like
this, nothing that good could happen to me."

"Vic Rood." I told him the address. "By now he'll
have moved his stock out of the place. But maybe he forgot some of it. Look under the cushion of his living-room
sofa."

I bought a fresh shirt on my way to the Miller Building.
I didn't want to go to the Miller Building. What I wanted
was to get on the *Straight Pass* and head for blue water—
and forget the whole damned mess. But I steeled myself

against it. There was a five-thousand-dollar bonus waiting for me, dimly seen through a fog of unanswered questions.

In the men's room on the fifth floor of the Miller Building I shaved, washed, and changed to the new shirt. Then I went to my office and called Chief Patrick in Mayport. I filled him in on what had happened, and asked if there was any word from or about Rita Kosterman. There wasn't. She'd vanished as thoroughly as Catleg.

I hung up and sat thinking about Kosterman's missing wife for a time. Finally, I phoned Anne Archer at her hotel.

"Hi!" she said when I told her who I was. "I was wondering how you were getting along." She sounded different, more relaxed and cheerful than at any time since I'd met her. "Keeping out of jail?"

"It's touch and go," I told her. "Have you by any chance heard from Rita Kosterman last night or today?"

"No. Why?"

"Just fishing for information."

"Oh? Well, I have some for you. About *me*. My husband flew down from Detroit last night—repentant and eager for a reconciliation. And here's another surprise for you. I'm *not* getting a divorce. He's a louse. But if there's one thing I've learned down here, it's that so are *all* men, one way or another. So I've decided, what the hell, why not keep the louse I've got."

"Sounds sensible," I admitted.

"I've a hunch," she said happily, "that Miami Beach is going to be a much nicer place for a second honeymoon than it was for waiting for a divorce."

I wished her the best of luck.

Next, I put through a call to Nate Feldman in New York.

"I ain't had any sleep since you called me yesterday," Feldman said when I got him on the phone. "If you tell me you've been fishing all this time, I'll shoot myself."

I said, "I've been having a grand time. What've you got for me?"

"Well, not the whole story yet on any of them. But here's what I've got. Nothing on any guy named Catleg.

On Jules Langley, the cops say he was working a racket with some call girls. Selling jewelry to their men friends. The men'd give the girls the jewelry; the girls'd give it back to Langley for a commission."

"I know about that," I told him. "What else?"

"Nimmo Fern, formerly Joe Furman, had some call girls working through him a couple years back for a while. His girls were some of the ones working the racket with Jules Langley. That's Nimmo's connection with Langley. All the connection I've turned up so far."

"How about Rita Nielsen?"

"Her I've got practically nothing on. Except through what I heard about Nimmo Fern. But I'd guess she knocked around quite a bit before she married him."

"Say that again?"

He said it again. "But that was five years ago. She walked out on him without a word about four years ago. Ain't been heard from since, far as I know."

"Anything else?" I asked absently, thinking about Rita and Nimmo. Suddenly, most of the questions had answers.

"One more thing," Foldman told me. "You asked me to try to get you Nimmo Fern's present Miami address. I got it."

It was a lovely Mediterranean-style white cottage with a red tile roof, set like a jewel in a lush green, palm-shaded garden on one of the causeway islands in Biscayne Bay.

Night was cloaking the bay when I reached it.

There was light showing through one of the big windows.

I walked on the grass, making no sound as I reached the side of the cottage. I moved along the wall to the edge of the window that showed light and peeked inside at a large, beautifully furnished living room built on several levels around a massive stone fireplace.

There was only one person in that room. Rita Kosterman. That didn't surprise me. She sat slumped in a deep chair, staring into the dark, empty mouth of the fireplace.

I shifted away along the wall, around the corner of the cottage, looking into the other windows, listening. I saw no sign of anyone else inside.

But I kept my hand on the gun in my jacket pocket as I rang the front door chimes.

Rita Kosterman opened the door. She had a gun in her hand, pointed at me. Her eyes were wide when she opened the door, her face grimly expectant. When she saw me, her eyes went a little wider; expectancy changed to disappointment.

"Hello, Mrs. Kosterman," I said gently. "Is Nimmo here?"

It took her a moment to recover enough to shake her head. "No," she whispered. Her hand holding the gun sagged.

I stepped inside, brushing past her. I put my hand on the door, and when she let go of it, I closed it.

"Waiting for Nimmo?" I asked softly.

"Yes," she said in a curious monotone.

I held out my hand toward her gun. "Better give me that, Mrs. Kosterman," I said carefully.

She backed away quickly. But the gun was no longer pointed at me. She was just holding onto it. "No," she said. "I'm going to kill him."

"Are you that sure Nimmo's the one who tried to get Kosterman killed?"

"Nobody else had any reason to." She moved away from me cautiously to the chair in which I'd first seen her. She lowered herself into it wearily, holding the gun in her lap, watching me to make sure I didn't take it from her.

I sat on the arm of a couch, facing her. "Tell me about it."

She looked at me emptily, not answering.

"Then suppose I tell it," I said. "It starts with the fact that you're not really Kosterman's wife. He doesn't know you were already somebody else's wife when you married him. Joe Furman, alias Nimmo Fern, is still your husband legally. You never got a divorce from him."

"I couldn't," she said flatly. "And it didn't matter,

anyway. I *was* Rudy's wife, except for some legal fine print. It didn't hurt anybody."

"Not until Anne Archer brought Nimmo out to your place for a party some five months back," I said. "That was the bit of wild bad luck that tore it for you. You'd run out on Nimmo, because you were afraid if he found out about Kosterman he'd ruin it for you. That's why you didn't get a divorce from Nimmo; he'd have found out why you wanted it. It worked fine for you until Nimmo came out to The Island that day and found you in a bigamous marriage with Kosterman."

I waited for her to say something. She didn't. She just sat looking at me, holding onto the gun on her lap.

I went on: "So Nimmo started blackmailing you. He knew Jules Langley from New York, which gave him a perfect way to collect from you. If you'd started trying to slip him big hunks of money, Kosterman would have gotten curious and found out. This way he didn't. You just began turning over all the jewels to Nimmo. And Langley had the phonies put in. Nimmo pocketed the profits from the real stones and split with Langley. It was a perfect setup for them. The gems weren't even hot because no one knew they'd ever been stolen.

"No one ever *would* have known either. But then your stepdaughter went out on a binge and lost that daisy pin. You saw it was missing when I brought Diana home and you put her to bed. You got scared and called Miami. Nimmo or Langley?"

"Nimmo," Rita whispered.

"Uh-huh. And he contacted Langley, who got real upset. Because he and Nimmo were all set to profit *double* from those jewels by having you toss them in the drink and declare them stolen. Then Kosterman'd replace the jewels with the insurance money, and the switching of phony stones for the real ones could be done all over again. Right?"

She nodded, staring at me with feverish eyes.

"Langley got worried that the daisy pin with the fake stones would turn up sometime, and ruin the setup," I went on. "So he set out to find the pin. First with Oscar. When they didn't find the pin on me, he called you and told you what to do. You sent Diana to me to hire me to turn up the daisy pin. And when I went out to try to locate it, Nimmo was tailing me. With a killer named Catleg."

Rita's shoulders were sagging. All the fight seemed to be draining out of her. "I don't know any Catleg. But the rest is true," she said tonelessly. "What the hell's the use. . . . I knew it was all bound to come out. I've been waiting for everything to fall in on me ever since Anne brought Nimmo out to the house. There's only one thing I want now."

"To kill Nimmo?"

She nodded.

"Why're you so sure he's the one who hired Kosterman to be shot?"

"Who else would have a reason? Nimmo must have started thinking about all the money I'd inherit with Rudy dead. And I'm still Nimmo's legal wife. He must have been planning to use that to blackmail most of Rudy's money away from me. And it's all my fault he tried it. If I'd told Rudy the truth in the very beginning . . ."

She told it all to me then, in a torrent that had been dammed up four years too long: "I led a lousy life before I met Nimmo in New York. I'd gotten to hate being on my own, alone. Nimmo was exciting, charming. . . . I thought it would be different being married to him. It was. It was worse. When he started pimping for a bunch of call girls, he even tried to get me to be one of them. . . .

"Then I met Rudy. He fell for me, wanted to marry me. No questions asked about my past. I was still Nimmo's wife. But I was afraid to go to him for a divorce. He'd have gotten curious and found out about Rudy. He'd have told Rudy about some of the things I'd done during my lousy life. Or blackmailed me the way he finally did. So I just went ahead and married Rudy and came down here. I thought no one would ever know. I hardly ever came into Miami, where I might run into somebody I knew from the past. I stuck pretty much to home. And it worked out well for me. For almost four years . . .''

"Until Nimmo Fern showed up," I said.

She nodded, her eyes filled with hate and misery. "Yes . . . after almost four years . . . I'd changed a lot in those four years, Rome. When I married Rudy, it was because he was a nice guy and could give me security and a chance for a decent life. But then I got to love the guy. Really love him. And I was happy because I knew I was being a good wife to him. . . . And then Nimmo came back into my life, threatening to ruin it completely, blackmailing me with the jewels as the payment.

"He never let me get out from under my fear that he'd ruin my life with Rudy. He even got a little photostat made of our marriage license and carried it in his wallet. He'd threaten to give it to Rudy if I got out of line—he even made me come here to him a couple of times by using that as a threat. . . .''

She was silent then. And so was I. Because now the last question was answered.

The marriage license in Nimmo's wallet.

Without that it had seemed that only Rita stood to gain by Kosterman's death. And through her, Nimmo. Now that was changed.

Now I knew who'd wanted Kosterman murdered. And where Nimmo was. And where to find Catleg.

I stood up. Rita quickly raised the gun off her lap, afraid I was about to snatch it from her.

"Put it away," I told her. "You aren't going to need it after all."

"What?" She blinked at me, not understanding.

"Wait for me," I said. "I'll be back for you."

Chapter 21

IT WAS LIKE EXPERIENCING ALL OVER AGAIN THE FIRST night I'd come to Boyd's ruined estate. Everything was the same—the darkness, the silence, the high crumbling brick wall overgrown with vines. And somewhere inside lurked Dr. Boyd's brother, Sam—who could find a man in the dark and stalk him silently.

Like the first time. Except that this time I knew he was in there.

I entered through the broken iron gate, making no effort to spot Sam; knowing I couldn't if I tried. Instead, I moved swiftly toward the hulking, decaying French château in the middle of the estate, following the same path as the last time. Pushing through the high tangle of weeds, I found the broken flagstone path and followed it to the abandoned swimming pool surrounded by the immense shapeless hedges. I could detect no sign that Sam was stalking me. But I banked on the probability, and just hoped he didn't decide to jump me before I was set for him.

Slipping through the hedges, I climbed the overgrown incline to the dark front of the hulking, sagging mansion. The smells of the decay and mold inside came out to me through the smashed windows. I halted in front of the window I used to enter the last time, as though I intended to use it again.

Then, I made a sudden thing of striding past it and around the corner of the building. Two steps around the corner I stopped, whirled, and dragged from the bulging right-hand pocket of my jacket one of the items I'd brought with me.

It was one of Nimmo's socks, loaded with wet sand and pebbles. It made an effective blackjack.

I had the heavy little sandbag raised above and behind my shoulder when Sam came noiselessly around the corner after me. He stopped short when he saw me standing there waiting for him. I didn't give him time to think. I swung the weighted sock as hard as I could.

It made very little sound as it slammed off his temple. His eyes rolled up in their sockets and his legs buckled. He fell down on his hands and knees. I bent and hit him again, behind the ear. He went all the way down and lay motionless.

It took me a moment to get my breathing back under control. I'd been more frightened than I'd let myself know. Kneeling beside his unconscious form, I got the roll of adhesive tape out of my other pocket, used strips of it to gag him and bind his wrists and ankles securely together behind him.

Leaving the loaded sock beside him, I straightened, took my gun from its belt holster, and continued around the abandoned mansion toward the cottage behind it.

Lights showed through two of the windows in the front of the cottage, and the front door was slightly ajar. I stopped and listened tensely. There was no human sound, anywhere. I moved silently to one of the lighted windows, looked in. I found myself looking into the living room of what had once been the tastefully furnished servants' quarters. The furnishings were still the same, but the place was disordered and badly in need of a cleaning job.

The only one I could see in the room inside was Lorna Boyd, Diana's mother. She lay face down on the living-room couch, one forearm lying on the floor beside a half-empty liquor bottle, breathing harshly and heavily through her open mouth.

Raising the gun a little in my hand, I went to the front door, pushed it all the way open. I took one step inside, then waited. There was still no sound, other than what came from Lorna Boyd. I drifted across the worn rug to the couch, touched her with my free hand. She didn't move. The tempo of the harsh breathing of her drunken sleep didn't change. I didn't have to bend down to smell the liquor on her breath.

Quietly, slowly, I went through the rest of the cottage interior. There was no one else inside it. Lorna Boyd was still in oblivion when I returned to the living room. I stepped out of the cottage, stood for a while studying the rear of the empty mansion.

Finally, I saw it—a faint gleam of light in one of the windows. The window of the room in which I'd tangled with Sam, the last time I'd come there. I remembered the bed in that room. There'd been no dust on top of it. There'd been stains on the sheet that could have been dried blood. . . .

I retraced my steps around the mansion, pausing when I reached Dr. Boyd's brother. He was still unconscious. I went on, to the front of the dark, looming building. At the window I'd used as an entrance the previous time, I stopped and took off my shoes. Leaving them behind, I climbed over the window sill.

This time I didn't have to use a flashlight. I remembered the route. Feeling my way cautiously, I moved through the dark maze of the decaying interior till I found the narrow, curving stairway leading upward. I began climbing it slowly, testing each step before trusting my full weight on it to make no sound. My hand was wet around the metal of my gun.

As I neared the top of the stairway, I saw the light from the bedroom ahead. I reached the second-floor hallway and slipped toward the light.

Through the open doorway of the room I saw that the light came from an oil lamp set on one side of the bed and a standing candelabra on the other side of it. Dr. Boyd was bending over the bed with his back to me, bandaging the chest of a man stretched out on the bed. The man on the bed was naked from the waist up. I couldn't see his face, but his narrow, short frame told me who he was.

A floorboard creaked under my foot as I stepped into the room.

Dr. Boyd straightened and jerked around to face me. His eyes went wide at the sight of me. Catleg—the man on the bed—came up on one elbow. The bandage was wide and bulky on his chest where my bullet had gotten him. His face was ashen and twisted with the pain of the wound. But when he saw me, he didn't hesitate. His movement was instinctive and instant. He grabbed up the .38 revolver that lay on the sheet beside him.

There was only one thing to do.

The explosion of the gun in my hand rocked against the walls of the room and brought a shower of plaster dust down from the ceiling. The gun slid out of Catleg's hand. He bent over sideways and fell off the bed to sprawl motionless in the tangle of shredding canopy material beside it.

I spun toward Dr. Boyd. He was dragging a small automatic from his pocket, but he stopped when he saw my gun aimed at him. Neither of us spoke as I took the automatic from his limp hand. His face was frozen. He stared at me and through me, at something far beyond that only he could see.

I turned and looked back down at Catleg. In death, he looked even smaller than he had in life. The hunt that had begun with finding Turpin's murdered body in my office was finished. I pictured Turpin laughing in Hell at all the trouble I'd gone through to avenge him.

Dr. Boyd said nothing all the way back to the cottage. Inside, his wife still lay lost in her alcoholic sleep on the couch. For all the attention he paid her, she might have been part of the furniture.

I used the rest of the adhesive tape I'd brought with me to bind him securely to a heavy, sagging wing chair. Then I left the cottage, got my shoes back on, and dragged Sam back to the cottage with me. It was quite a job. I was winded and perspiring when I finally settled him on the living-room floor leaning against the wall. His eyelids fluttered as consciousness seeped slowly back into his brain.

I checked the tapes around his wrists and ankles to make sure they'd hold him.

Then I used the cottage phone to call Art Santini at Miami homicide.

"Anthony Rome," I said when Santini came on the phone. "I'm ready to square myself with the department."

"That'll take some doing, Tony."

"Suppose I give you a doctor without a license who's been patching up wounded criminals? Redhanded. And along with him the guy that killed Ralph Turpin—who also happens to be a professional killer the cops want for a job six months old?"

There was a moment's silence at the other end of the line. Then Santini said quietly, "We might almost like you. I'm listening."

I told him where to come, and to bring some men with him.

After hanging up the phone, I settled in one of the living-room chairs, holding my gun on my knee while we waited. I looked at the three of them—Sam with his eyes wide open now, glaring at me, Lorna Boyd still out; Dr. Boyd lost in his bitter memories and thoughts of the future.

I thought of all the diverse lives you touch, once you dig beneath the surface of any single person's life. One life affects another, which in turn affects still another—on and on like a long chain of turning gears. People who have no knowledge of each other's existence, yet change each other's manner of life and time of death.

A nice, slightly spoiled daughter of a wealthy business-man lost a small piece of jewelry—and as a result a slum girl with a hunger for dope smashed to her death in a car crash.

A restless divorcee from Detroit met an unscrupulous gambler from New York—so a jeweler from Holland drowned in a bathtub.

A reasonless anger took hold of me as I sat waiting with the Boyds in that cottage. I was tired of other people's lives. I had a hunger to be alone in an empty world for a while. . . .

Santini had two uniformed cops with him when he arrived. He looked from me to the Boyds, then back at me—holding out his hand.

"All right," he snapped as I gave him my gun. "Tell me about it."

"That one," I said, pointing to Lorna, "is Mrs. Boyd. She had too much to drink, and she's been out like that since I got here. She doesn't know what's gone on around her." I nodded at Sam. "Be careful with that one." I explained about Sam.

Then I turned to the man I'd tied to the chair. He stared frozenly at the far wall, as though not part of any of this.

"This," I told Santini, "is the ex-Doctor Boyd. He got caught performing abortions and lost his license to practice. He's been making ends meet since then by handling things no honest doctor'll touch. Like patching up men who don't want their wounds reported to the cops. You'll find one of them in that mansion next door. He's wanted for killing a Miami gas-station owner six months ago. Called himself Catleg. I had to shoot him, in self-defense. You'll find his gun with him. I'll lay odds it's the one that killed Turpin."

"Well, well . . ." Santini said mildly.

"He followed Turpin up to my office—together with a New York gambler named Nimmo Fern. They had an argument with Turpin about something. Turpin went for his gun. Catleg shot him, but Turpin managed to squeeze his own shot off before he tapped out. It didn't hit Catleg though; it got Nimmo."

"Yeah? And where do we find this Nimmo?"

I told him, "You'll have to dig for him."

I picked up Rita Kosterman at Nimmo's villa and drove her back up to Mayport. On the way, I told her how I'd figured it. There was only one way it could be figured, once I'd found out about the photostat of the marriage license in Nimmo's wallet.

I'd known a lot of it before—up to the point where Turpin had taken Catleg's bullet, and put a slug into Nimmo before dying. Now the rest of the story had fallen into place.

Leaving my office after killing Turpin, Catleg had been dragging a badly wounded Nimmo with him. And he'd taken him straight to Boyd—whom he probably knew from having his hip patched up after that gas-station owner shot him. He got Nimmo to Dr. Boyd, but Nimmo had died of his wound before Boyd could do anything for him. That accounted for the fact that no one had seen or heard from Nimmo since Saturday morning.

So Boyd and Catleg had a corpse on their hands and had to get rid to it. The easiest thing would be to bury Nimmo somewhere on that overgrown estate. But first they went through Nimmo's wallet for whatever money he had on him. And they found that marriage-license photostat.

It didn't mean anything to Catleg. But it meant a lot to Boyd. He knew who Rita Nielsen was. And if Rita was really married to Nimmo at the time of her wedding with Kosterman, then she wasn't legally Kosterman's wife. Boyd saw in that a way out of his poverty.

If Kosterman were dead, it would take only an anonymous phone call to his lawyers to start them checking the New York marriage-license records. They'd find out that Rita was Nimmo's wife when she married Kosterman. And Kosterman's will left almost everything to his wife—which, legally, Rita was not.

Once Rita's bigamy was established, there was only one person left to inherit it all—Kosterman's daughter, Diana. And Lorna Boyd would have no trouble getting enough money out of her daughter for her and her husband to live the rest of their lives comfortably and decently. And they'd be safe. Rita might be suspected of the murder, but the Boyds would never even enter into the case.

So Dr. Boyd made a deal with Catleg to murder Kosterman. And Catleg would have succeeded if I hadn't happened to be there to yell a warning to Kosterman and scare Catleg off after that first shot. . . .

Rita Kosterman listened silently to the whole story I told.

When I finished, the first words from her were: "Then . . . Nimmo *is* dead?"

"Uh-huh. We found him buried under some bushes near the swimming pool. With a forty-five slug still in him."

She took a few moments more, absorbing it, believing it. Then she asked, shakily: "And how much of all this that you've told me do the police know?"

"Nothing about you," I told her. "They know Langley somehow managed to steal all the jewelry from your house and switch the gems. They know what happened between Catleg, Nimmo and Turpin, but not why. And they know about Boyd doctoring Catleg and Nimmo. They don't have any of the facts that connect any of those things with you. And with a little luck, that's the end of it."

I pulled the Olds up at the curb in front of the Mayport Hospital and looked at Rita. "Maybe you'd like to be the one to tell him the whole story," I suggested.

She nodded. "Yes . . . I should have told him long ago."

"Sure," I agreed. "Then there wouldn't be so much to tell."

After she went into the hospital, I headed for the corner diner, and breakfast. I gave it another hour. Then I phoned Art Santini in Miami.

"You're smelling better now," he said when I got him on the phone. "It was like you said. Catleg's thirty-eight checks with the bullet we took out of Turpin. And that slug in Nimmo Fern came from Turpin's forty-five."

He told me the rest of it. My luck—and Kosterman's—stayed solid. Boyd's twin brother, Sam, of course, couldn't tell the cops anything that helped them. Lorna Boyd was hysterically swearing she knew nothing of her husband's activities with criminals. And Boyd was maintaining a stony silence. He hadn't said anything about hiring Catleg to murder Kosterman. And he wasn't likely to. He was in enough hot water over his illegal practice without adding that.

"There's still a lot of things to be answered," Santini warned me. "Like why Turpin and Nimmo Fern and Catleg started shooting each other in your office."

"They must've disliked each other," I said.

"Dammit, Tony! That's not enough answer and you know it."

"It's all the answer any of us are likely to get," I told him. "They're both dead now. You've got no grounds for complaint. You've got the man who killed Turpin. And you've got a wanted killer-for-hire and an illegal doctor as a bonus. It will look good on your record. And in the newspapers. And I'm the one who turned it all up for you. Don't forget that. And don't let Captain Jones forget it."

"You're a pretty tricky guy," Santini rasped.

"Yeah," I said. "A real sneak player."

I hung up the phone and went to see Kosterman in his hospital room.

Rita sat in a chair beside his bed. They were holding hands and looking like blissful newlyweds enjoying the repentant aftermath of a lovers' quarrel.

"Rita has told me everything," Kosterman said. "I only wish she'd told me the truth when we first met. I'd have arranged her divorce from this man Fern. It seems the ones I love best are always keeping things from me. Darrell. Diana. And now Rita. I wish I knew why."

I passed on to them what Santini had told me.

"Well," Kosterman murmured, "there's one good thing that's come of all this. With Fern dead, there's nothing to interfere with Rita and me having a quiet remarriage somewhere." He smiled faintly at Rita and squeezed her hand.

"There's one more thing you can do while you're tying up loose ends," I told him. "Lorna, your ex-wife, claims she knew nothing about Boyd's illegal doctoring of criminals. A good lawyer shouldn't have much trouble making that stick. I'd suggest you hire a lawyer for her. For your daughter's sake. And then I'd suggest that you see to it Diana's mother doesn't have to go on living the way she has been. It would take a weight off your daughter. Then maybe she'll be able to concentrate better on her own problems. She won't have to go on a binge every time her marriage suffers a normal upset."

Kosterman nodded slowly. It came hard for him, but he said it: "I know I was wrong about that. . . . I'll do it."

"That's it, then," I said, straightening, feeling weights of my own beginning to drop away from me. "It's still in the family, the way you wanted it. If your luck holds, it'll stay that way."

"Thank you," Kosterman said. "I'll be sending you a check. That bonus I promised you."

"You do that," I said, turning to leave. "I earned it."

I was crossing the rough water over the reef when dawn spread across the sea. I turned my head and looked back from the wheel of the *Straight Pass* at Miami. It looked beautiful—a long line of tiny, shining white buildings edging the sea, their towers tinted rose by the rising sun, the long thin strip of golden sand below them. From that far out, you couldn't see all the beasts that crawled through that beauty.

I kept sailing out to open water, heading north of Bimini.

An hour later there was no land in sight anywhere around me.

About the Author

Marvin H. Albert was born in Philadelphia and has lived in New York, Los Angeles, London, Rome, and Paris. He currently lives on the Riviera with his wife, the French artist Xenia Klar. He has two children, Jan and David.

He has been a Merchant Marine Officer, actor and theatrical road manager, newspaperman, magazine editor, and Hollywood script writer, in addition to being the author of numerous books of fiction and nonfiction.

Several of his books have been literary Guild choices. He has been honored with a Special Award by the Mystery Writers of America. Nine of his novels have been made into motion pictures.